Between Time and Timbuktu is an experimental television script composed mainly of bits and pieces of stories written by Kurt Vonnegut over the past twenty years. It tells the story of Stony Stevenson, winner of a competition for which the prize is a journey into the chronosynclastic infundibulum, or time warp, where Stony's perceptions of time and space are shattered to smithereens. This book is a unique example of Kurt Vonnegut's special blend of scientific expertise, wit, and penetrating comment, and should not be missed by anyone with a taste for science fiction, unusual imagination or excellent humour ...

By the same author

Player Piano
The Sirens of Titan
Mother Night
Cat's Cradle
God Bless You, Mr Rosewater
Slaughterhouse-Five
Welcome to the Monkey House
Happy Birthday, Wanda June
Breakfast of Champions
Wampeters, Foma and Granfalloons
Slapstick or *Lonesome No More!*
Jailbird
Palm Sunday
Deadeye Dick

Between TIME and TIMBUKTU

or Prometheus-5

A SPACE FANTASY
BASED ON MATERIALS BY

Kurt Vonnegut

DESIGNED BY JOEL SCHICK
WITH PHOTOGRAPHS BY
JILL KREMENTZ
AND FROM THE
NET PLAYHOUSE
PRODUCTION

GRAFTON BOOKS
A Division of the Collins Publishing Group

LONDON GLASGOW
TORONTO SYDNEY AUCKLAND

Grafton Books
A Division of the Collins Publishing Group
8 Grafton Street, London W1X 3LA

First published in Great Britain by
Grafton Books 1975
Reprinted 1986

Published by arrangement with
Delacorte Press/Seymour Lawrence
New York, N.Y., U.S.A.

Copyright © Kurt Vonnegut, Jr. and Educational
Broadcasting Corporation 1972
Photographs copyright © Jill Krementz 1972

ISBN 0-586-04141-9

Printed and bound in Great Britain by
Collins, Glasgow

Set in Times

All rights reserved. No part of this publication
may be reproduced, stored in a retrieval system,
or transmitted, in any form, or by any means,
electronic, mechanical, photocopying, recording or
otherwise, without the prior permission of
the publishers.

This book is sold subject to the condition that
it shall not, by way of trade or otherwise, be
lent, re-sold, hired out or otherwise circulated
without the publisher's prior consent in any
form of binding or cover other than that
in which it is published and without a similar
condition including this condition being
imposed on the subsequent purchaser.

CAUTION: This script in its printed form is designed for the reading public only. All dramatic rights in it are fully protected by copyright and no public or private performance—professional or amateur— may be given without the written permission of the author and the payment of royalty. As the courts have also ruled that the public reading of a play constitutes a public performance, no such reading may be given except under the conditions stated above. Anyone disregarding the author's rights renders himself liable to prosecution.
Communications should be addressed to the author's representative, Farber & Siff, 230 Park Avenue, New York, New York 10017.

Cast
(IN ORDER OF APPEARANCE)

Stony Stevenson
WILLIAM HICKEY

Contest Announcer
BRUCE MORROW

Mrs. Stevenson
DORTHA DUCKWORTH

Walter Gesundheit
RAY GOULDING

Bud Williams, Jr.
BOB ELLIOTT

Col. Donald "Tex" Pirandello
FRANKLIN COVER

Sandy Abernathy
RUSSELL MORASH

Dr. Bobby Denton
JOHN DEVLIN

Bokonon
KEVIN MC CARTHY

Island Girl
EDIE LYNCH

Soldier
JERRY GERSHMAN

Dr. Paul Proteus
JAMES SLOYAN

Prosecutor
GEORGE SERRIES

Deaf Juror
ASHLEY WESTCOTT

Drunk
JOHN PETERS

Miss Martin
HELEN STENBORG

Dr. Hoenikker
HURD HATFIELD

General
DOLPH SWEET

Lead Caroler
HARRIET HAMILTON

Policeman
SAM AMATO

Diana Moon Glampers
BENAY VENUTA

First Stagehand
CARLTON POWER

Larry
JEAN SANOCKI

News Announcer
JACK SHIPLEY

Ballerina
ALEXIS HOFF

Harrison Bergeron
AVIND HAERUM

Short Order Cook
FRANK DOLAN

Nancy
SUSAN SULLIVAN

Lionel J. Howard
CHARLES WHITE

Announcer
PHILLIP BRUNS

Wanda June
ARIANE MUNKER

Hitler
PAGE JOHNSON

Cemetery Gardener
MC INTYRE DIXON

This book is based on the
television script of the
NET Playhouse production,

Between
TIME
and
TIMBUKTU

A SPACE FANTASY

Kurt Vonnegut, Jr., was
commissioned to be an advisor
on and contributor to the script
in 1971 and the program was first
aired nationally on public
television stations on March 13,
1972. Many good people created
funny stuff as the filming
progressed, most notably Bob
Elliott and Ray Goulding, and
Fred Barzyk, the director. The
first draft of the script, most
of which survived, was by
David O'Dell.

Preface

This book is said to have been written by me. And I *did* write it, too, pretty much—over the past twenty-two years. But it would never have occurred to me to put my words in this particular order. That vision was received by some friendly people at National Educational Television in New York and at WGBH in Boston. With my permission, they took unrelated incidents from several of my stories, and they tacked them together to form a rough draft of a script for a ninety-minute TV show.

I was reminded of the bizarre surgical experiments performed in the H.G. Wells tale *The Island of Dr. Moreau*. Dr. Moreau cut up all sorts of animals—and he assembled grotesque new creatures from the parts.

I began to fool around with the script myself. I grafted the head of a box turtle onto the neck of a giraffe, so to speak—and so on. Amazingly, chillingly, hilariously, the impossible creature lived for a little while. It was clumsy, funny-looking, and almost pathetically eager to please.

It had a soul, too, which was mainly supplied by an extraordinarily gifted actor my own age, William Hickey. Bill played the part of the reluctant astronaut, Stony Stevenson. Since Stony was not a strongly motivated character, and since we weren't sure what he was supposed to represent anyway, we asked Bill to be himself. He demonstrated that Bill as Bill, adrift in time and space, was an enchanting human being.

Hello, Bill.

My father loved the music of Kurt Weill, and he said one time, admiringly, that the music sounded as though it were written by an inspired amateur. My father was a professional architect. I think he came to resent the neatness and tightness and slickness which his professionalism (and his clients) imposed on his designs. He could never be slapdash or childish or passionately crude. He could never do what inspired amateurs did, which, among other things, was to leave a lot to Lady Luck.

This script, it seems to me, is the work of professionals who yearned to be as charming as inspired amateurs can sometimes be. True, we hired the finest actors and technicians we could find. As for the meaning of the show, though, we left that to Lady Luck. She was good to us this time.

We shot first and asked questions afterwards, which is the American way. It was a picnic. It was a lark. I have never had more skilful, amusing associates.

While we were filming the show, usually on weekends, I told other writers, "Hey, get into non-commercial television." I said this only to writers who were rich. "The pay is lousy," I said, "but the freedom is total, as nearly as I can tell. They'll get you almost any actor you want, they'll break their necks to create any effect you want, and the writer has as much authority as Alexander the Great."

I still feel that way.

As for myself, though, I am not going to have anything more to do with film—for this reason: I don't like film.

I love National Educational Television. I love

WGBH of Boston, which had so much to do with the making of this film. I love George Roy Hill and Universal Pictures, who made a flawless translation of my novel *Slaughterhouse-Five* to the silver screen. I drool and cackle every time I watch that film, because it is so harmonious with what I felt when I wrote the book.

Even so—I don't like film.

Film is too clankingly real, too permanent, too industrial for me. As a stingy child of the Great Depression, I am bound to complain that it is also too fucking expensive to be much fun. I get the heebie-jeebies every time I hear how much it will cost to fix a scene that doesn't work quite right. "For God's sake," I say, "leave it just like it is. It's *beautiful!* Leave it be!"

I have become an enthusiast for the printed word again. I have to be that, I now understand, because I want to be a character in all of my works. I can do that in print. In a movie, somehow, the author always vanishes. Everything of mine which has been filmed so far has been one character short, and the character is me.

I don't mean that I am a glorious character. I simply mean that, for better or for worse, I have always rigged my stories so as to include myself, and I can't stop now. And I do this so slyly, as do most novelists, that the author *can't* be put on film.

Every deeply felt novel which has been turned into a movie has, as a movie, seemed one character short to me. It has made me uneasy on that account. I suspect that the audience has been vaguely uneasy, too—for the same reason.

The worst thing about film, from my point of view, is that it cripples illusions which I have encouraged people to create in their heads. Film doesn't create illusions. It makes them impossible. It is a bullying form of reality, like the model rooms in the furniture department of Bloomingdale's.

There is nothing for the viewer to do but gawk. For example: there can be only one *Clockwork Orange* by Stanley Kubrick. There are tens of thousands of *Clockwork Oranges* by Anthony Burgess, since every reader has to cast, costume, direct, and design the show in his head.

The big trouble with print, of course, is that it is an elitist art form. Most people can't read very well.

Well, so much for film as compared with print. As a friend said of another terrific theory of mine: "It has everything but originality."

I might as well say something about the filming of my play *Happy Birthday, Wanda June*. It was one of the most embarrassing movies ever made, and I am happy that it sank like a stone.

It was all the director's show, which is usually the case. So was *Slaughterhouse-Five*. That's fine, as long as the director is a great director. George Roy Hill is a great director.

I had nothing to do with the script of *Slaughterhouse-Five,* incidentally. That was the work of Steven Geller—and a good job it was. I didn't meet him until after the picture opened. He is a novelist, too, and I asked him which he liked best, writing novels or screenplays. He preferred novels by far, since they were wholly under his control.

I told him what Bill Hickey, my actor friend, had said to me about writing for the legitimate theater or the screen, in effect: "Be prepared to direct what you write, or forget it. If you're going to write something but not direct it, you'll be doing only half your job."

Which is true.

I would like to say something about American comedians: they are often as brilliant and magical as our best jazz musicians, and they have probably done more to shape my thinking than any writer. When people ask me who my culture heroes are, I express pious gratitude for Mark Twain and James Joyce and so on. But the truth is that I am a barbarian, whose deepest cultural debts are to Laurel and Hardy, Stoopnagel and Bud, Buster Keaton, Fred Allen, Jack Benny, Charlie Chaplin, Easy Aces, Henry Morgan, and on and on.

They made me hilarious during the Great Depression, and all the lesser depressions after that. When Bob Elliot and Ray Goulding agreed to work on this TV show, I nearly swooned. I would have been less in awe of Winston Churchill and Charles de Gaulle.

I wrote some of their jokes in this script, and they delivered them gracefully. But they also made up a lot of new stuff, even when the cameras weren't operating, which made me laugh so hard that I thought I would go through the rest of my life wearing a truss.

One of them said this about Stony Stevenson's mother: "She certainly has nice manners for a welfare deadbeat." When they were asked out of the blue what an astronaut's favorite food was out in space, there was no hesitation. The prompt answer was, "Dehydrated artichoke hearts." And so on.

Cheers.

**Between
TIME
 and
TIMBUKTU**

CONTEST ANNOUNCER

Good day, America. . . . At last, the day we're going to announce the grand prize winner in the Blast-off—Blast-off, as you know, the space food of the astronauts—the Blast-off Space Food Jingle Contest. Behind me, in this house, is the winner. The winner does not know that he has won the Blast-off contest. May I please have the bottle . . . thank you, Miss Blast-off.

MISS BLAST-OFF
Here you are.

CONTEST ANNOUNCER
Lovely, lovely. Now . . . this is an exciting
moment. . . . I'm a little nervous, it's been so
many months. LADIES AND GENTLEMEN!
THE WINNER IS . . . Mr. Stony Stevenson,
12 Harrison Boulevard, Indianapolis, Indiana.
. . . AND NOW, MR. STEVENSON,
HERE WE COME!

[*Music up full*]

[CONTEST ANNOUNCER *knocks on door*]

CONTEST ANNOUNCER
Just think, ladies and gentlemen, in a few
moments from now in this typical modest
American home, in this modest American
community, you will meet the man who has won
the Blast-off Space Jingle Contest, the energy
drink of the astronauts and Mission Control.
We're going to present him with the grand prize, a
trip to the Chrono-Synclastic Infundibulum. Here
he comes now. . . .

MRS. STEVENSON
Yes?

CONTEST ANNOUNCER
Excuse me, madam . . .

MRS. STEVENSON
Oh, no thank you, we don't want any.

 [MOM *starts to shut door*. CONTEST ANNOUNCER *knocks again*]

CONTEST ANNOUNCER
Madam, excuse me. . . . You don't understand. May I just speak to you for a moment? We are on network television right now.

MRS. STEVENSON
Oh!

CONTEST ANNOUNCER
Is this the home of Mr. Stony Stevenson?

MRS. STEVENSON
Yes. . . .

CONTEST ANNOUNCER
Well, may we see him please? We have a *very* important announcement.

MRS. STEVENSON
STONY!

VOICE OF STONY
WHAT DO YOU want, ma?

MRS. STEVENSON
SOMEBODY here for you. . . .

CONTEST ANNOUNCER
In a few moments, ladies and gentlemen, the magic of live television, the excitement . . . Here he comes now, here he comes. . . .

STONY

[*Quietly, meekly*]

Oh, hi.

CONTEST ANNOUNCER
Hello, good day to you. . . . You are Mr. S. Stevenson?

STONY
Yes, that's right . . . Stony Stevenson.

CONTEST ANNOUNCER
Stony Stevenson, CONGRATULATIONS! Pardon me, mama. We have an important announcement to make to you right now. YOU ARE THE WINNER, THE GRAND PRIZE WINNER in the Blast-off Space Jingle Contest. . . . AMERICA, HERE'S YOUR WINNER— STONY STEVENSON!

[*Flashbulbs go off. March music starts up. Cheering crowd*]

[STONY *is led from the house to a car*]

MRS. STEVENSON
Stony!! Stony, come back!

[STONY *in car, looks back toward* MOM]

Between TIME and TIMBUKTU

A SPACE FANTASY
BASED ON MATERIALS BY

Kurt Vonnegut, Jr.

GESUNDHEIT
This is Walter Gesundheit

WILLIAMS
and ex-astronaut Bud Williams, Jr.

GESUNDHEIT
bringing you every exciting moment of the Flight of Prometheus-5, direct from Mission Control Space Flight Center.

WILLIAMS
Right.

GESUNDHEIT
Three months ago Mr. Stony Stevenson received the news on nationwide TV that he had won first prize in the Space Poem competition.

WILLIAMS
Quite a thing.

GESUNDHEIT
Yes it is. And since then he has undergone one of the most concentrated crash courses for astronauts ever devised and in a very few moments we will see the results of these endeavors. Prometheus-5 with Astronaut Stony Stevenson

aboard is on the launching pad and with you we will wait out the final moments before blast-off.

WILLIAMS
Really is tense here today, Walter. . . .

GESUNDHEIT
Right, Bud. Tense is the word of the hour as Astronaut Stony Stevenson sits high atop the rocket awaiting his launch into the Chrono-Synclastic Infundibulum.

WILLIAMS
Walter, I understand we have contact with Astronaut Stevenson in his capsule now. . . . Why don't we find out just what he's thinking in these last few moments before blast-off.

[*Cut to Rocket Ship sitting quietly on launching pad*]

GESUNDHEIT
Good thinking Bud. . . . Come in Stony Stevenson. . . . Astronaut Stevenson . . . this is Walter Gesundheit and ex-astronaut Bud Williams . . . can you hear us?

   [*Long pause, then nothing but noise and interference on the monitor*]

WILLIAMS
Can you hear him, Walter?

GESUNDHEIT
Can't even see him. . . . Sorry, it seems we have some difficulty with the connection to the space capsule. For those of you who just tuned in, the countdown for the launch of Prometheus-5 has been temporarily halted at zero minus sixty

seconds. Bud . . . you were on Prometheus-1 and
Prometheus-3.

WILLIAMS
That's right, I was.

GESUNDHEIT
What I really wanted to ask was . . . how did a
highly trained technical person like yourself feel
when you learned that a man who writes poetry
in his spare time was going to make this trip?

WILLIAMS
At first, I felt he would be too emotional, Walter.
I thought, Maybe he can give us some fancy
descriptions of things, but if the going really gets
tough, the way it did on Prometheus-3 . . .

GESUNDHEIT
You mean, when the Tang got loose in the
landing module . . . ?

WILLIAMS
There was Tang all over the place, and no
gravity. But when I realized that they were going
to put a man right through a time warp, a
Chrono-Synclastic Infundibulum, I said, "Well
. . . maybe only a poet could describe a thing
like that."

GESUNDHEIT
Words somehow seem inadequate when one is
describing space.

WILLIAMS
Yes, if you remember, I had a great deal of
trouble describing Mars.

GESUNDHEIT
You said it looked like your driveway back home in Dallas.

WILLIAMS
Yes, that's what it looked like to me at the time. So, if they were to put me through a time warp—

GESUNDHEIT

  [*Aside*]

A Chrono-Synclastic Infundibulum . . .

WILLIAMS
—right—I probably would be speechless myself.

GESUNDHEIT
Um.

WILLIAMS
I mean . . . you put a man through a time warp—

GESUNDHEIT

  [*Aside*]

A Chrono-Synclastic Infundibulum.

WILLIAMS
—and for a while he's going to be scattered not only through space but time! He's going to be a hundred places at once, and there's no way of guessing just where, you know.

GESUNDHEIT
Bud . . . what kind of training has Astronaut

Stevenson gone through to prepare for this mission?

WILLIAMS
Walter . . . he's really trained very hard for the mission. You know we have a standard here at Mission Control . . . standard of excellence.

GESUNDHEIT
That's the atmosphere here at Mission Control, Bud . . . excellence.

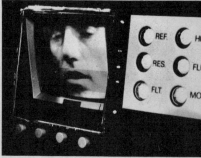

[*Cut to flashing control panel. Truck past sea of wires and connectors. CU of finger pushing switch . . . word next to it says "Flush." CU of sweating brow. CU of eyes as they move from left to right.*]

WILLIAMS

It takes a special person, one with fortitude . . .
ambition, skill, intelligence, forthrightness,
awareness, and most of all guts to work here in
the heart of Mission Control. It's here that the
very life of Astronaut Stevenson will be watched
over and cared for, where his every heartbeat,
respiratory and digestive activity will be monitored
by computer. Excellence is the byword and the
product of this crack team here at Mission Control.

GESUNDHEIT

I understand that we have now made contact
with Stony Stevenson high atop his launch rocket.
Hello, Stony.

   [*A lot of noise and a vague picture of Hopalong
   Cassidy riding across the screen of the monitor,
   then more noise*]

GESUNDHEIT

Yes, and it takes a special kind of a man to be a
space adventurer, an explorer of the unknown, a
man from Mission Control is very special indeed.

   [*Music, rich and full*]

VOICE OF TEX

Geologist.

Physicist.

Electrical Engineer.

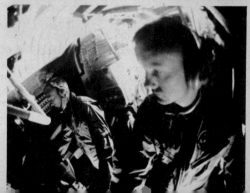

Physician.

Chemist.

Test Pilot.

The Air Force.

The army and the navy.

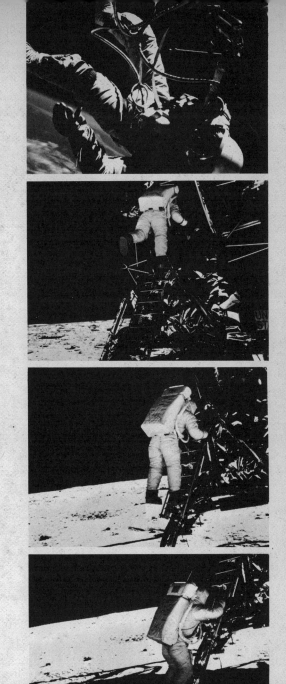

And now the poet, Stony Stevenson.

One and all, the great team . . .

THE MEN FROM MISSION CONTROL

GESUNDHEIT
Before we hear from our astronaut we are fortunate to have Mrs. Stevenson, Stony's mother, with us in the studio. She has been keeping up a constant vigil here at Mission Control. Bud . . .

WILLIAMS
You must be very proud of your son.

MRS. STEVENSON
It doesn't seem possible. Nobody in our family ever won a contest.

WILLIAMS
Well, I'd like to announce to you and to the American public that Stony was made an honorary private in the United States Army this morning.

MRS. STEVENSON
Isn't that something!

WILLIAMS
Isn't that great?

MRS. STEVENSON
Uncle George won't believe it . . .

WILLIAMS
When he was a child, did you have any intimation that someday he would be going off into space like this?

MRS. STEVENSON
He used to be interested in the pressure cooker. He would get it out and play with it, seal it up tight, and then unseal it again . . . put different things in it . . . marbles, his toy fire engine. . . .

WILLIAMS
Um.

MRS. STEVENSON
Now they got *him* all sealed up.

WILLIAMS
I was about to say that he came from a typical American family, but of course he's not a typical American astronaut, is he?

MRS. STEVENSON
Depends on what kind of typical you're talking about. I think we're typical Americans. His father committed suicide. I've been married three times . . . happily only once.

WILLIAMS
To Stony's father.

MRS. STEVENSON
To Fred K. Bonzer.

[*Silence*]

WILLIAMS
Stony did grow up, though, in the American Middle West . . .

MRS. STEVENSON
Indianapolis.

WILLIAMS
In what we could consider a typical Hoosier house . . .

MRS. STEVENSON
The welfare people had us in a Holiday Inn for a while. That was quite a scandal.

WILLIAMS
Why do they call people from Indiana Hoosiers? I've often wondered about that.

MRS. STEVENSON
Nobody knows.

[*Silence*]

WILLIAMS
So Stony Stevenson's roots are in Indiana soil.

MRS. STEVENSON
He has a cemetery lot in Brooklyn, New York.

WILLIAMS
Pardon me?

MRS. STEVENSON
Fred K. Bonzer, my third husband, inherited a cemetery lot in Brooklyn from a rich uncle. He gave it to Stony on Stony's eighth birthday. . . .

WILLIAMS
Um.

   [*Silence*]

MRS. STEVENSON
At a big party at the Holiday Inn.

WILLIAMS
Um.

MRS. STEVENSON
That was before the newspapers found out the welfare people had put us up there at thirty bucks a night.

WILLIAMS
Right.

MRS. STEVENSON
That was just before the
   [*Bleep*]
hit the fan.

WILLIAMS

Are you signaling me, Walter?

GESUNDHEIT

Sorry to interrupt, Bud. Let's switch now to Colonel Donald "TEX" Pirandello, the voice of Prometheus-5. Tex, I know there's been a lot of conversation about will he wear his space suit or won't he. Do you have a final decision on that?

[TEX *at mission control desk*]

TEX

Right, Walter . . . soon after launch he will take off his outer protective envelope or space suit and eject it from the capsule. He will not need his space suit in his travels. . . . Astronaut Stevenson will drink orange-flavored hydrogen peroxide, and absorb the slowly released oxygen through the wall of his small intestine. Communications between the capsule and Mission Control will be established momentarily. In the meantime, I know he would want me to let everybody know how happy and proud he is today. He's raring to go. We are at sixty seconds and counting.

GESUNDHEIT

Oh, my.

[*Nervous laugh*]

We interrupt this countdown to bring you special coverage of a disturbance at South Gate. Take it away, Sandy.

[*Scene changes to* SANDY *at south gate in crowd of protestors*]

SANDY ABERNATHY

This is Sandy Abernathy at the South Gate of Mission Control. The radical evangelist Dr. Bobby Denton and a group of his avid followers are protesting the launching of Prometheus-5 It's an angry crowd and the guards cannot hold . . .

TEX
Minus forty-five seconds.

SANDY ABERNATHY

Dr. Denton was just released yesterday from federal prison where he had served a nine-day sentence for disorderly conduct for his actions at the Poor People's March last June.

WILLIAMS
Thirty seconds and counting.

SANDY ABERNATHY

They have refused to leave. Let's take a listen.

DENTON

These scientists, I say, are just building another tower of Babel. We don't need them and we don't need their countdowns to get us where we're going, do we?

CROWD

No!

DENTON

Because we have our own countdown here on God's green spaceship. You know what it is?

CROWD

No!

DENTON

Do you want to hear it?

CROWD

Yes!

DENTON
TEN!

VOICE FROM MISSION CONTROL
Ten . . .

DENTON
Do you covet thy neighbor's things?

CROWD
No!

VOICE FROM MISSION CONTROL
Nine . . .

DENTON
Nine! Do you bear false witness?

CROWD
No!

VOICE FROM MISSION CONTROL
Eight . . .

DENTON
Eight! Do you steal?

CROWD
No!

VOICE FROM MISSION CONTROL
Seven . . .

DENTON
Seven! Do you commit adultery?

CROWD
No!

VOICE FROM MISSION CONTROL
Six . . .

DENTON
Six! Do you kill?

CROWD
No!

BUD and WALTER
Five . . .

DENTON
Five! Do you honor thy father and mother?

CROWD
Yes!

TEX
Four . . .

DENTON
Four! Do you keep the Sabbath?

CROWD
Yes!

TEX
Three . . .

DENTON
Three! Do you take the Lord's name in vain?

CROWD
No!

BUD and WALTER
Two . . .

DENTON
Two! Do you make any graven images?

CROWD
No!

TEX
One.

DENTON
BLAST-OFF!

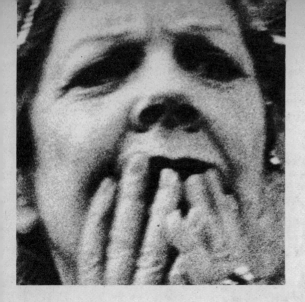

MRS. STEVENSON
Oh!! Blast-off!!

[*Cut to Rocket Ship sitting quietly on the launching pad . . . nothing happens, then . . .*]

GESUNDHEIT
Blast-off.

VOICES FROM MISSION CONTROL
Absolutely no reading . . . No . . . That's it.
Hold it. . . . All right.

   [*Rocket Ship blasts off*]

TEX

It's all systems go. . . . Prometheus-5 has cleared the tower. . . . It's a good one . . . delta acceleration at maximum . . . optimum burnout projected . . . cabin tracking locked in . . . looks good from here.

GESUNDHEIT

Well, there you had it . . . the successful launch of Prometheus-5, a historic day as man reaches farther into space to find the meaning of life. Traveling at twenty-eight thousand miles an hour Stony Stevenson is headed for the Chrono-Synclastic Infundibulum. And it is in that time warp where Astronaut Stevenson may find the answer to all creation.

> [*Scene changes to celebration at Mission Control. Chorus sings "For He's a Jolly Good Fellow." Noises of celebration, champagne flowing*]

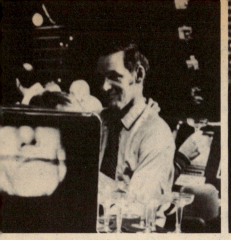

GESUNDHEIT (*Voice Over*)
What did you think of Astronaut Stevenson and the launch of Prometheus-5, Bud?

WILLIAMS (*Voice Over*)
Well, I thought he did real fine, Walter, and this launch certainly couldn't be called a lemon . . . no, sir . . . it's no lemon.

WILLIAMS
They're really having a great time, aren't they?

GESUNDHEIT
They're really pleased.

WILLIAMS
They deserve it, too.

GESUNDHEIT
Really pleased.

GESUNDHEIT

[*Laughs*]

They're really pleased.

WILLIAMS
They deserve it.

[*Chorus sings "For He's a Jolly Good Fellow."*]

GESUNDHEIT

[*Laughs*]

We could stand some of that bubbly ourselves.

[*Staff of mission control make a toast to* STONY. *Music up. Dissolve to lonely Rocket Ship in space*]

TEX
All indicators point favorably. Respiration, heartbeat, blood pressure, oxygen, water, cabin pressure, all indicate A-OK.

STONY

   [*Quietly, emerging from shock*]

Then, I'm not dead . . .

TEX
Oh, no—you're just fine . . . you're just fine. We do get an excess moisture reading for the upper module of your space suit.

STONY
Yeah. Me, too.

TEX
You have a simple explanation?

STONY
Yeah.

TEX
Could we have it, please?

STONY
I think I threw up.

TEX

   [*Laughs*]

Hey, o dog-gone it, we've lost him.

JULY

[*Music up, then fades slowly*]

TEX
You have one hundred and twenty million miles to travel and according to latest calculations you should reach the Chrono-Synclastic Infundibulum in three months, four days, thirteen hours, three minutes, and seven seconds.

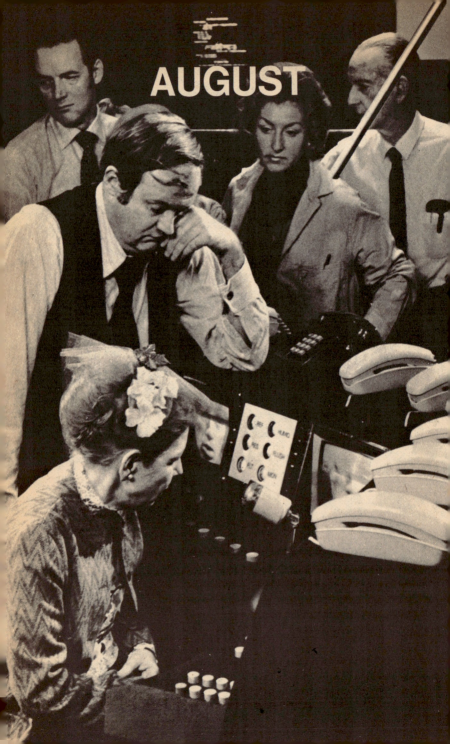

AUGUST

[*Music up again, then fades*]

MRS. STEVENSON
Stony . . .

STONY
Ma? Is that you? It's good to hear a familiar voice, ma.

MRS. STEVENSON
You're a very brave boy, Stony. I'm very proud of you . . . and so is your Aunt Alice, and Cousin Bruce. Mrs. Meyers from next door says you come to dinner when you come back from your trip.

STONY
That's real nice of her, mom.

GESUNDHEIT
I see Mom Stevenson's still in Mission Control, Bud.

WILLIAMS
That's right, Walter. She's moved right in.

GESUNDHEIT
A mother standing by her son in his moment of need.

WILLIAMS
She's moved a cot in the back of the retro readouts and she's put doilies on the backs of all the chairs.

GESUNDHEIT
A marvelous woman, Bud.

[*Music*]

TEX

You want to tell us if you plan to write any more poetry?

STONY

Yes, my first one is going to be a sestina, I hope.

TEX

Well, a sestina. All I know about poetry is Burma-Shave.

STONY

A sestina has six stanzas with six lines each . . . and the same six words and the lines of every stanza, you see, but in different order each time. The six words I've chosen are taken from man's words when he set foot on the moon: "One, long, step, for, man, kind." The order of the end words in the second stanza will be, "Long, one, man, kind, step, for." And then in the third stanza it is to be, "For, step, kind, man, one, long." In the fourth stanza it will be "Step, kind, for, one, long, man."

OCTOBER

NOVEMBER

GESUNDHEIT
Merry Christmas, this is Walter Gesundheit . . .

WILLIAMS
and Bud Williams, Jr.

GESUNDHEIT
bringing you the continuing saga of Prometheus-5. Private Stony Stevenson is approaching the core of the time warp at a speed of twenty-eight thousand miles an hour.

Silent Night
Holy Night . . .

TEX
He's fading . . . he's fading . . . I've lost him, I've lost him.

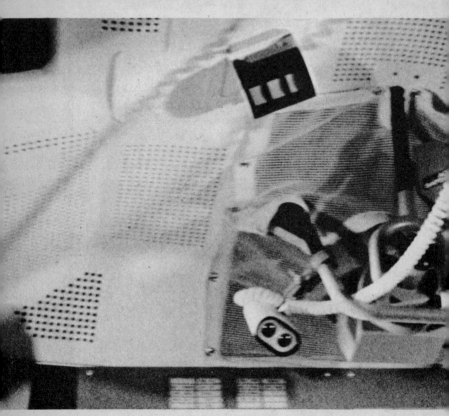

GESUNDHEIT

It is now six months since Stony Stevenson blasted off on his epic adventure. Communications have become increasingly hard the farther he moves away from earth. But the moment has arrived by all our calculations when Stony will hit the Chrono-Synclastic Infundibulum. . . .

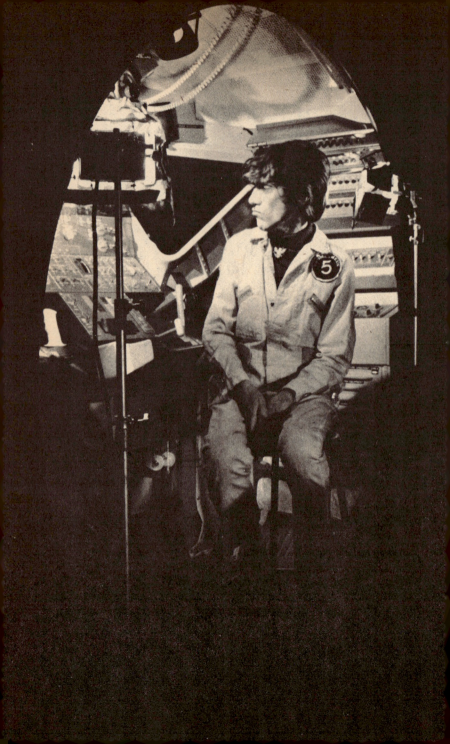

GESUNDHEIT
He could be anywhere and everywhere. . . .

[*Rocket Ship falls faster and faster, breaking into flames. We hear a faint scream. Colors . . . Swirls . . . Blobs moving and dancing . . .* STONY *flapping arms, distorted as if his molecules were disorganized.* STONY *six images run across the screen . . . three in sync and of different colors and the other three out of sync, but also in various colors. Music . . . Dixieland dance piece.* STONY *emerges again . . . this time doing a dance with himself.*]

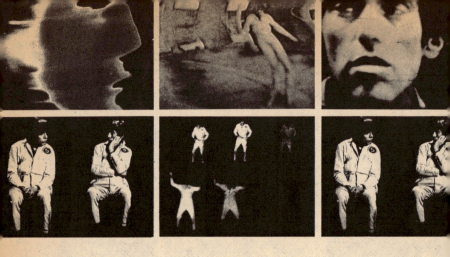

STONY I
Who are you?

STONY II
I was just going to ask you the same thing.

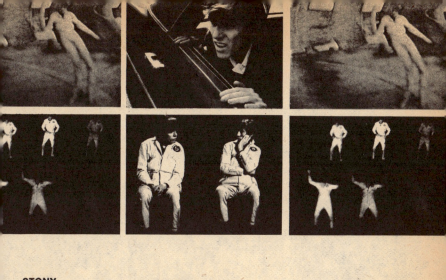

STONY

This is a mistake. . . . Oh, what a terrible mistake.

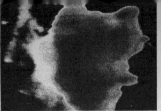

MRS. STEVENSON
Stony, can you hear me? Can you hear me, son?
This is mother.

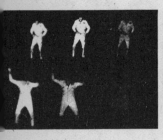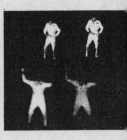

STONY I
Did they tell you to expect this?

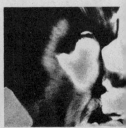

STONY II
They told me I might come straight back to earth
in the present or the future, not the past.

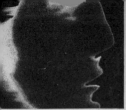  

STONY I
The past, the past . . . oh, the past . . .

GESUNDHEIT
I guess nobody knows now when we'll see Corporal Stevenson again.

WILLIAMS
No, if ever . . .

 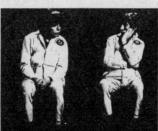 

[*Picture goes black, then find body of* STONY *laying on beach on the Island of San Lorenzo*]

STONY
Am I dead yet?

GESUNDHEIT
I understand that Stony's writing a poem out there in space, Bud.

WILLIAMS
Oh, really?

GESUNDHEIT
Yes, and he's chosen those immortal words first spoken by man when he stepped on the moon.

WILLIAMS
Those words are very patriotic, Walter.

GESUNDHEIT
"One step for man . . ."

WILLIAMS
No, I think it was, "A giant step for man, a long leap for mankind."

VOICE OF STONY
Am I dead yet?

WILLIAMS

"One long step for mankind . . . ?"

GESUNDHEIT

No, it was, "One step onto the moon for man . . ."

WILLIAMS

"Moon" wasn't in there, Walter. Not in that . . .

GESUNDHEIT

"One step"—wasn't it?—"for man, and two steps for mankind."

WILLIAMS

"One step for man, and two steps for mankind?" It doesn't flow the way it did originally.

GESUNDHEIT
"I'm stepping now for man . . ."

WILLIAMS
I think you have it now.

GESUNDHEIT
". . . hoping that all mankind will remember this moment . . ."

WILLIAMS
". . . in history."

GESUNDHEIT
Did he say "two steps" at all?

WILLIAMS
No, it was, "One step for man and one for mankind." I . . . does anybody . . . ?

[STONY *is welcomed by people of San Lorenzo*]

BOKONON
Welcome to the island of San Lorenzo. Does that make you happy or sad?

STONY

[*Looking around*]

That depends, I suppose.

BOKONON
A wise answer. We fished you from the sea. Are you all right?

STONY
I think so.

BOKONON
Good.
Allow me to introduce myself—I am Bokonon,
author of the *Books of Bokonon*.
These are some of my pupils.

STONY

My name is Stevenson. Call me Stony.

BOKONON

I am very interested to meet you. I suspect we may belong to the same karass. You see, I myself was washed ashore on this island forty-seven years ago. It was the major *vin-dit* of my *sam ah ki bo*.

> [BOKONON *holds up book in his hand*]

I see you are not a Bokononist. Come, I will teach you.

> [*Music, band, and voices singing a calypso number*]

Tiger got to hunt,
Bird got to fly,
Man got to sit and wonder,
Why, why why?

Tiger got to sleep
Bird got to land
Man got to tell himself
He understand.

BOKONON

The people, these children of mine, are practicing *bakomaru,* a gentle form of lovemaking . . . nonviolent lovemaking. Be happy, my children . . . Bokonon is watching over you.

BOKONON
We Bokononists believe that humanity is organized into teams, teams that do God's will without ever discovering what they are doing. Such a team is called a karass. You are here, doing God's will, not knowing exactly why you are doing it. . . . You and I are members of the same team . . . the same karass. Welcome to the team.

STONY
Thank you.

BOKONON
When I was washed ashore on this island, I found a people almost crushed by poverty and political repression. Now, I have given them a religion of harmless lies, and you can see how happy they are.

STONY
How can a useful religion be founded on lies?

BOKONON
When the truth of your life is too terrible, that truth becomes your enemy.

   [*Noise of helicopters*]

STONY

   [*Running and yelling*]

What is it?

BOKONON

   [*Plowing through underbrush*]

I forgot to tell you, my religion has been outlawed. The government is trying to kill me.

Don't worry. It happens all the time.

[*Natives are pursued—narrowly escaping from the invaders*]

SOLDIER
Come on now, where are you? Come on, where'd everybody go? I think we got 'em on the run now. Where are you guys hiding? Ugh, first I get mosquitoes and then I lose . . .

BOKONON
All right, my children. I think we're safe for the moment.

> [STONY, BOKONON *and girl native hide in bush*]

STONY

> [*Still whispering*]

Excuse me, Mr. Bokonon. Why is your religion outlawed?

BOKONON
It was my own idea. I thought it would give the religious life of the people more zest, more tang. It did, in the beginning.

STONY
And then?

BOKONON

[*With a troubled scowl*]

The president was my friend. He agreed to play along. It was like a game, really. We agreed the penalty for practicing the religion would be death . . . on the hook.

STONY
Um.

BOKONON
No one was supposed to be killed. It was all threats and rumors. And then . . . the president and I drifted apart.

STONY
Were you very close?

BOKONON
He was my best friend. We had made a play, a work of art, of our life on the island. He would play the cruel tyrant in the city, and I the gentle holy man in the forest. It was an innocent make-believe—to distract the people from their miserable existence. Everything was fine, until . . .

STONY
Until people started really being . . . executed?

BOKONON

[*Nods sadly*]

Yes.

[*Pauses for reflection*]

[*Sad music*]

I suppose that it goes to show that you have to be
very careful what you pretend to be . . .
because one day you may wake up to find that's
what you are.

[*A swirling* STONY *image recedes into black oblivion*]

STONY
Oh—Oh!

VOICE OF ISLAND GIRL
He disappeared!

VOICE OF BOKONON
Yes . . . but I think he stayed as long as he could.

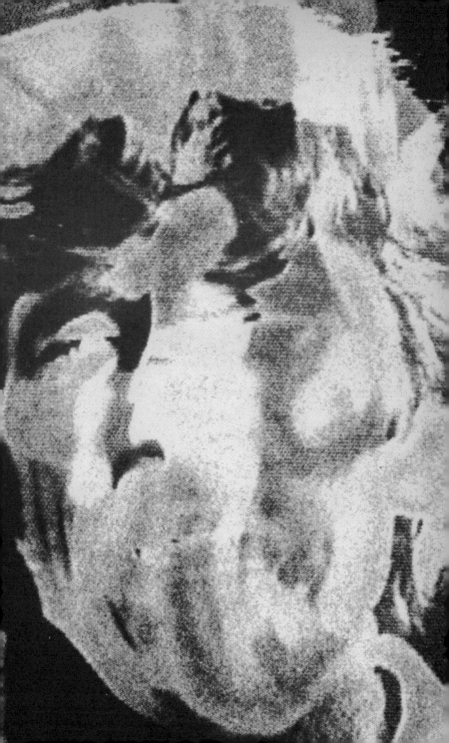

[*Back at Mission Control*]

GESUNDHEIT
"One step for mankind, and a . . ." That's funny, I . . .

VOICE OF STONY
Wait! Will you wait?! Wait!

WILLIAMS
. . . my driveway reminded me of Mars.

GESUNDHEIT
Yeah.

WILLIAMS
I don't think I ever pointed out that my driveway back home is red.

GESUNDHEIT
Well, that could be it then, right.

WILLIAMS
A lot of people have been kidding me about that, and I didn't point out that it is red.

GESUNDHEIT
I wasn't kidding you.

WILLIAMS
I know that, but we think of Mars as red, and that's why . . .

GESUNDHEIT
Well, let me ask you one thing. Was it a red driveway when you bought the house?

WILLIAMS
Yes, it's been red as long as I've known the place. It came that way. Quite a few in that neighborhood are red driveways, as a matter of fact.

GESUNDHEIT
Isn't that an unusual color for a driveway? I don't mean to harp on the subject, but—why don't you change it?

WILLIAMS
I had no particular reason to change it. I don't think we need to make a big point out of it.

GESUNDHEIT
No, I don't think it's very important.

[*Slow fade on film shot of* MAN
*running . . . long telephoto lens
. . . man starts walking fast . . .
then almost runs . . . breaks into
run . . . running as hard as he can,
running forever toward the camera
in desperation. Slow motion.*

*Overemphasized sound of his
breathing . . . as he runs faster it is
almost gasping. He is crying in fear
. . . We also hear heart beat.*]

PROSECUTOR

State versus Dr. Paul Proteus . . .
graduated after Second Industrial Revolution . . .
summa cum laude engineering and
 management . . .
rumored underground with revolutionary Gray
 Shirt Society . . .
captured last week attempting to destroy Illium
 control computer.

[*Voice echoes*]

You have pleaded guilty of conspiracy to commit sabotage, to fomenting a riot, and to crossing state lines unlawfully. Do you still deny you are guilty of armed insurrection and treason?

[*Cut to gavel pounding . . . the sound echoes forever . . . dissolve*]

[*Music*]

[*CU of wires being attached to skin. CU of pin piercing skin. CU of electrodes put on finger. CU of electrode attached to ear lobe. CU of mike attached to heart area . . . bare chested.*]

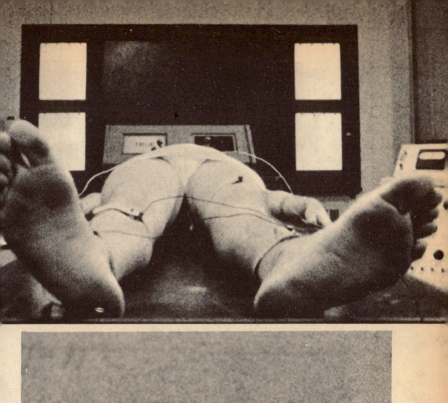
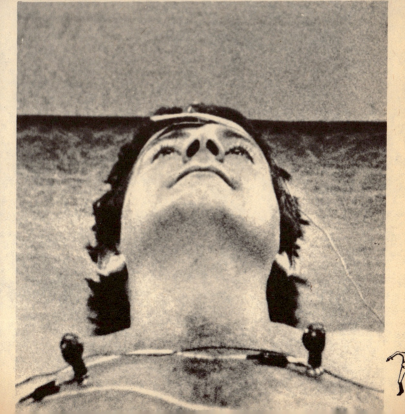

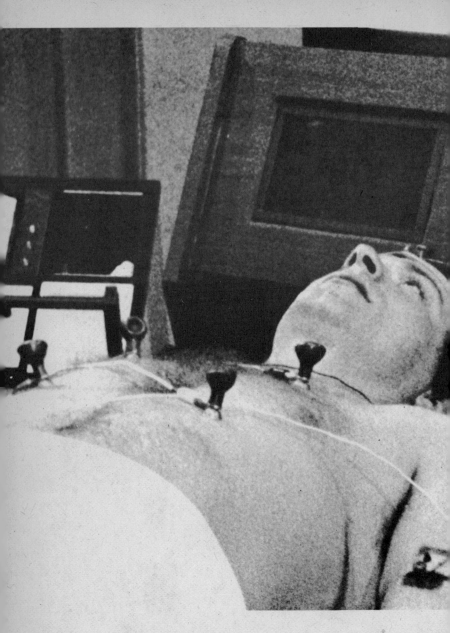

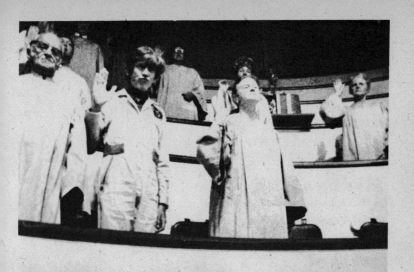

[*Defendant lies on a table strapped to electronic lie detector gear. Jury stands with raised hands,* STONY *among them*]

Do you solemnly swear in all causes between party and party that shall be committed unto you, you will solemnly render true verdict according to the law and evidence, so help you God!

JURY
So help me God!

STONY
So help me God!

PROSECUTOR
You may sit down. . . . This use of force—you don't regard that as levying war against your country, as treason?

DR. PAUL PROTEUS
The sovereignty of a country resides in its people, not in its technology. We are vigilantes, waging war on a lawless technology in the name of the people.

PROSECUTOR
Who are you anyway, a crackpot patriot or a power hungry revolutionary?

DR. PAUL PROTEUS
I only want what's best for my country.

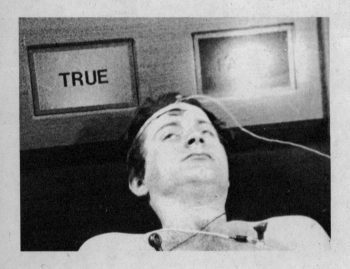

PROSECUTOR
A half-truth. What's the whole truth?

DR. PAUL PROTEUS
It is the truth.

   [*Jury members are talking among themselves*]

PROSECUTOR
Quiet, quiet!

DR. PAUL PROTEUS
I demand an audit of this machine.

[*Jury members break out into excited conversation*]

PROSECUTOR'S VOICE
Order, order. The court truth technician will please check the lie detector circuits.

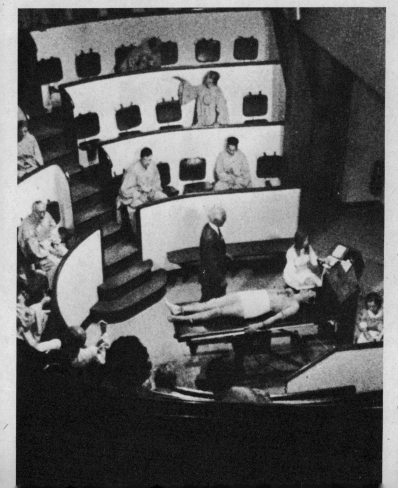

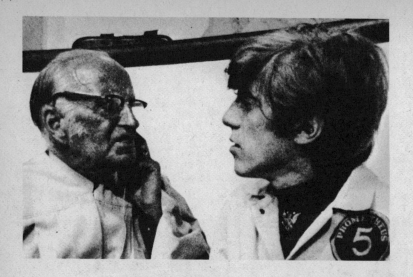

STONY

Excuse me. Do you know what's going on here?
What is he yelling at him for? What did he do?
What century is this? Is this earth?

DEAF JUROR

   [*Wearing a hearing aid*]

You better ask somebody else. I miss a lot . . .
need new batteries.

STONY

Right . . . sorry.

DEAF JUROR

They ask me if I'm in favor of capital punishment,
but they don't ask if I hear or not.

   [*Laughs*]

STONY
Your Honor . . .

PROSECUTOR

[*Coming over to* STONY]

What's this?

STONY
Would you tell me the date, please, sir.

PROSECUTOR
Where's your gown? Didn't anybody tell you to wear a necktie and a business suit and a gown when serving on jury duty?

STONY
No, sir.

PROSECUTOR
If you appear tomorrow dressed like this, I'll hold you in contempt of court. We have a man on trial for his life here, and you come dressed like a member of the lower classes. How would you like to be tried by a member of the lower classes?

STONY
I'd hate it very much.

PROSECUTOR
Get a haircut!!!

STONY
Sir, won't you please tell me what date this is?

PROSECUTOR
Why would you interrupt the business of the court to ask a question like that?

STONY
I thought it might be my birthday.

PROSECUTOR

   [*Shouts in disbelief*]

Your birthday?!!

DEAF JUROR
Birthday? I love birthdays!

   [*Sings and jury members join in*]

Happy birthday to you, happy birthday to you.
Happy birthday dear juror . . .

PROSECUTOR
Quiet! Quiet! Now let's get down to business.
Lower the screen. Here is state evidence item
number thirteen.

   [*Screen is lowered behind defendant*]

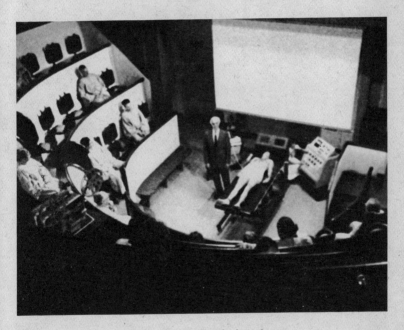

In this unbiased essay we will see the fruits of our
great society. This is the same society that the
defendant wishes to destroy. This is the same
society that is paying you for jury duty today. It
is indeed a land of plenty.

   [*An animated movie is shown*]

ANNOUNCER
It's a good life, isn't it . . . John Averageman? But did you ever stop to think what makes it such a good life for you and your loved ones? Well, the answer's easy—it's modern technology and our industrial system.

JOHN
Those are pretty big words. What do they mean to me, an average guy?

ANNOUNCER
Well, John, perhaps I can show you. John, our automated industrial system has made you richer than Caesar . . .

Napoleon . . .

and Henry VIII put together.

Remember, for all his gold and armies Charlemagne could not have gotten one single transistor radio. Not to mention the insurance, health, and retirement benefits you get through your employer, John.

JOHN
I never looked at it that way. Gosh! Sort of makes you think, doesn't it?

ANNOUNCER
But that's not all, John. Under this system our civilization has reached the dizziest heights of all time! Far beyond the wildest dreams of our past.

  [*The "Battle Hymn of the Republic" is heard, softly at first but slowly rising in volume*]

Thirty-one point seven times as many television sets as the rest of the world put

together. Seventy-seven percent of the world's automobiles. Eighty-three percent of all the world's air conditioners.

[*Shouting now, to be heard above music*]

Eighty-five percent of its power lawn mowers.
Ninety-six percent of its helicopters.
Ninety-eight percent of its snowmobiles.

Ninety-nine point nine percent of the world's . . .

[*Voice drowned out by music*]

PROSECUTOR
Well, I hope the jury was paying attention to that.

[*Cut to* JURY . . . *Some sleeping, others knitting, some playing cards,* STONY *looking bored.*]

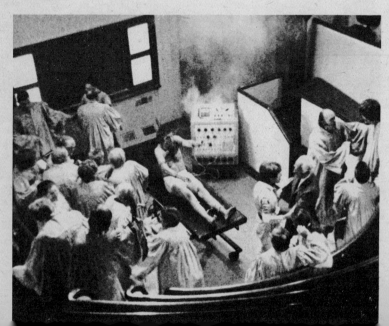

Cut to JURY *as the green smoke starts to choke them . . . most of them screaming.*

STONY *works his way past screaming old people . . . Bumps into the* PROSECUTOR *who yells at him over the crazy sound of the machine destroying itself and the Defendant screaming.]*

Pull the plug . . . For Heaven's sake . . . pull the plug . . . pull the plug.

[*Machine destroys itself in billows of green smoke.* STONY *finds cord and trails it around in smoke and screaming people.*]

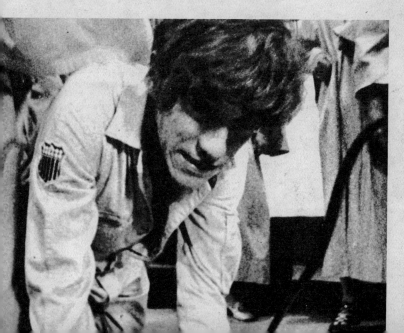

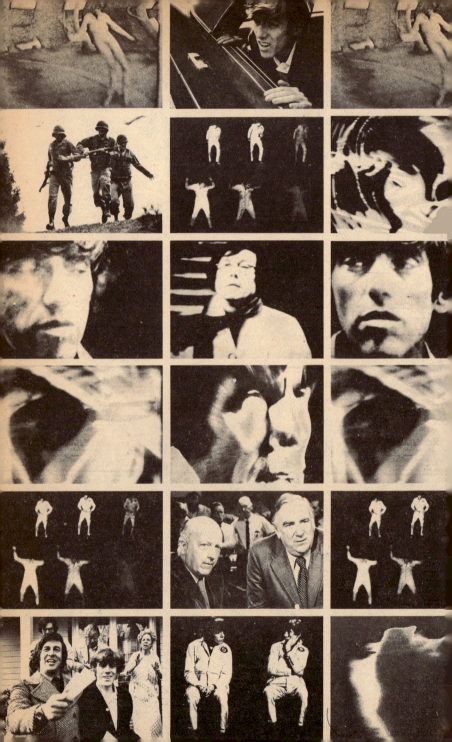

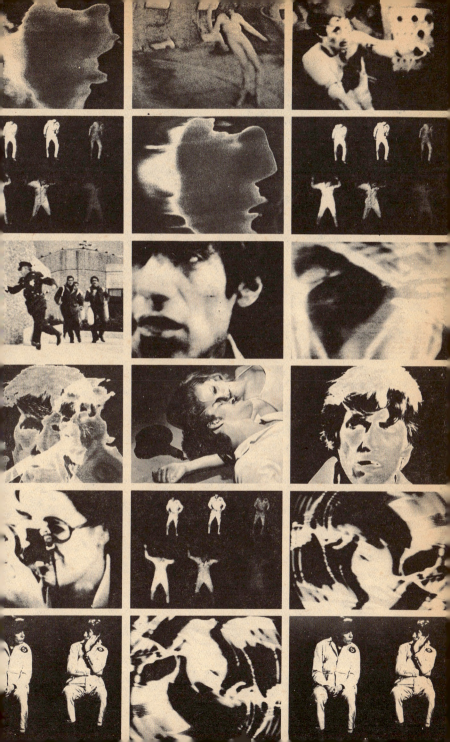

[*Scene changes to* STONY *on sidewalk asking for a dime. Only a drunk stops to listen.*]

STONY

Excuse me, excuse me. Could I have a dime for a phone call, please. Miss, excuse me, please . . . I wanted to ask you something. I'm an astronaut and I have to call Mission Control. You see, they thought of everything but a dime . . .
 Could you spare a dime for a man who's been shot through a Chrono-Synclastic Infundibulum?

A DRUNK

  [*Heartbrokenly*]

That is the saddest story I ever heard in my life.

[*He gives* STONY *all his change, spilling money all over the sidewalk.*]

That is the saddest story I ever heard in my life.

STONY
Thanks a lot. Thank you very much.

A DRUNK
Boy, oh boy. That is the saddest story I ever heard in my life.

   [*Beginning to cry*]

That is the saddest story I ever heard . . . oh boy . . .

MAN FROM MISSION CONTROL
Hello.

STONY
Hi. Is Tex there, please?

MAN FROM MISSION CONTROL
Yeah. Just a minute.

[*To* TEX]

Tex, Tex, it's for you.

TEX
Tex here. Hello, who is this?

STONY
Me. Stony Stevenson.

TEX
STONY! Where the hell are you?!!

[*Mission Control staff starts talking excitedly*]

STONY
Well, it's . . . uh . . .

   [*Spelling name on telephone box*]

S-C-H-E-N-E-C-T-A-D-Y. Oh! Schenectady. I'm in Schenectady.

   [*Sudden panic at Mission Control as tracking system fails*]

EXCITED VOICES
Look! Something's gone haywire! Look! He's totally out of our tracking mechanism.

TEX
Private Stevenson!!

MAN FROM MISSION CONTROL
He's a corporal now.

TEX
Corporal Stevenson! This is an order. Everything

on Earth is completely off limits! Get back into
space!

STONY
Sir, I am not in control of my own destiny. It's a
miracle I can control my own bladder.

TEX

   [*To Mission Control staff*]

Listen! He's lost control. Does anybody here
know how to get him back into outer space?

   [*Excited babbling*]

Well, somebody better come up with a plan, and
soon!

   [*To* STONY *again*]

Corporal Stevenson! Is there any way you can
get the hell out of there and back into outer space?

STONY
Sir, what happens happens. I think that I'm
traveling through my own nightmares . . . and
a few nice dreams, too. Otherwise, why would
everybody I meet speak English? Why else would
everything be so American, when America is all
I've ever known?

   Oh, sir, there *is* something strange to report about
Schenectady. I mean not that everything isn't
strange about Schenectady. It seemed to be
summer a minute ago, and now everything's
frosting up. Oh, there's another thing. I suddenly
feel very sleepy, sir. Sir, I . . .

[*As snow covers the phone booth,* STONY *yawns, has trouble keeping his eyes open and falls asleep. Scene changes to* STONY *asleep on surgical table in meat locker*]

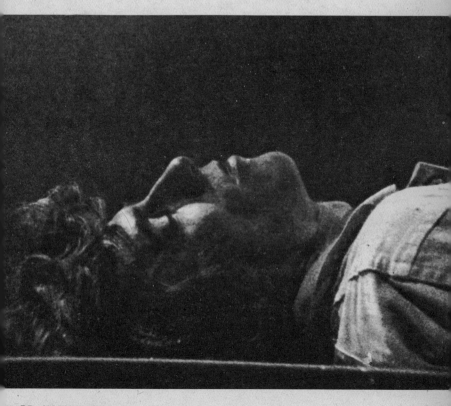

DR. HOENIKKER
I really don't understand, Miss Martin. . . . How could he have gotten in here?

MISS MARTIN
I really don't know Dr. Hoenikker. . . . It's a total mystery.

STONY

[*Waking up*]

Mama?

HOENIKKER
Are you sure he's an extra body?

MISS MARTIN
I checked and checked . . . they are all there . . . Truman Capote, Julius LaRosa, Henry Kissinger . . .

HOENIKKER
When he's thawed, bring him in and we'll see if we can find out who he is.

MISS MARTIN
Yes, doctor.

STONY
Mama?

MISS MARTIN
I'm not your mommy. All right, now. Sit up . . . that's my baby.

STONY
Boy. What phone service in Schenectady . . .

MISS MARTIN
Don't be afraid. This is the Hoenikker Laboratory of Immortality. Now stand up. That's the boy.

[*She helps him into a fur coat*]

Now that we've got you thawed out, we want to keep you good and warm.

VOICE
Dr. Saroyan, please call extension 308 in the sperm bank. Dr. Saroyan to the sperm bank please.

   [STONY *in wheelchair being pushed by* MISS MARTIN]

MISS MARTIN
Upsy-daisy, here we go.

[*Scene changes to* HOENIKKER & GENERAL *in lab with bodies in bags*]

GENERAL

Doctor, you must do it. . . . It's important. Dammit, Hoenikker, you know more about freezing than any other human being in history. I want you to figure out some way to freeze battlefields, so American soldiers will never again have to fight in mud.

DR. HOENIKKER

There's always winter, of course. A Russian winter is especially good. Why don't you declare war on persons who live in cold climates—Laplanders, Eskimos, Finns.

MISS MARTIN

We are now going into Dr. Hoenikker's laboratory. You mustn't be alarmed by what you see here. Dr. Hoenikker has helped good human beings who were about to die. He has preserved them until cures can be found for their diseases. He has frozen them into suspended animation.

GENERAL

Listen, doctor, if you can get a handle on this I can get you any amount of R and D money. We can set up a crash program tomorrow. What do you want? One million? Two million?

DR. HOENIKKER

So easy to get money for killing . . . and all I can do is scrape up just two or three thousand to freeze the best minds of our time.

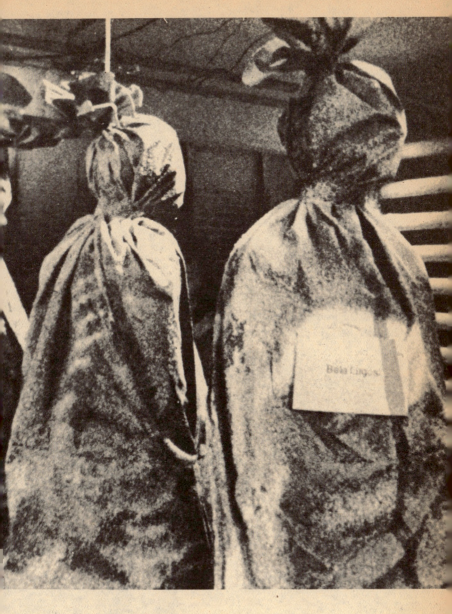

MISS MARTIN
Dr. Hoenikker is a wonderful man. He's very busy, but he wants to ask you a few questions. You're our mystery man, you know.

STONY

> [*Moaning*]

Oh . . .

> [MISS MARTIN *and* STONY *enter lab where* HOENIKKER *and* GENERAL *are talking*]

GENERAL
OK, sure it is easy to get money for defense. Damn right. Man is an infantry animal. There'll always be wars and the winning side will be the one who kills the most people on the other side. And everybody likes to be on the winning side, right?

DR. HOENIKKER
Um.

GENERAL
Right.

MISS MARTIN
Excuse me, doctor. Here we are.

DR. HOENIKKER
Ah, yes. Who are you?

STONY
The abominable snowman?

DR. HOENIKKER
Did you ever volunteer to be frozen here?

STONY
Not that I know of.

DR. HOENIKKER
Did you ever make a deposit in our sperm bank?

STONY
If I did, it was a small one.

[*Alarm bell*]

DR. HOENIKKER
What's that now?

MISS MARTIN
Oh, it's the girl pool.

GENERAL
The girl pool?

[*Girl pool enters singing "Joy to the World"*]

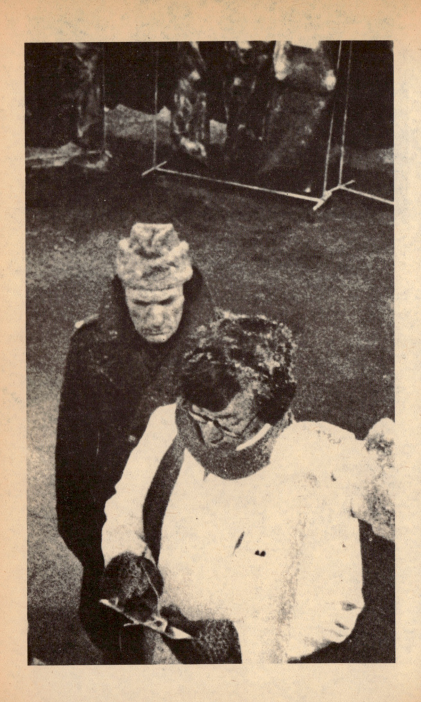

LEAD CAROLER
The girl typing pool from Building number three wish you and yours a very Merry Christmas. From Ann, Belinda, Joan, Glenda, Suzanne, and all the girls in the typing pool.

DR. HOENIKKER
Merry Christmas.

   [*Girl pool begins singing "O Little Town of Bethlehem"*]

GENERAL

   [*Whispers*]

Doctor, can we get back to the problem?

DR. HOENIKKER
I have been thinking about it. Now I suppose that there are many ways in which water could freeze. All ice forms, you see, around the nucleus, a seed, we call it. Now suppose that there were one seed with a melting point of say, a hundred and forty degrees Fahrenheit. Now we would call that Ice Nine.

   [*Girl pool begins singing "Jingle Bells"*]

   [*To girl pool*]

Oh, shush!

   [*They continue, but very quietly*]

GENERAL
What's this got to do with my problem?

DR. HOENIKKER
You see general, a melting point of one hundred and forty degrees makes anything below that hard as a rock.

GENERAL
I'm beginning to see the point.

DR. HOENIKKER
Precisely. Mud.

STONY
Mud?

DR. HOENIKKER
The general wants to attack mud. It's the infantry's stickiest obstacle. Just picture the marines in a quagmire, a godforsaken swamp . . . with their trucks and tanks and howitzers all wallowing, sinking in stinking miasma and ooze. What do they do?

STONY
Use helicopters?

DR. HOENIKKER
Supposing one soldier had with him a tiny capsule containing a seed of Ice Nine. . . .

STONY
Ice Nine?

DR. HOENIKKER

[*Nodding head with enthusiasm*]

And suppose that soldier threw that tiny seed into the nearest puddle . . .

MISS MARTIN
The puddle would freeze.

DR. HOENIKKER
And all the muck around the puddle?

STONY

[*Not sure he has the right answer*]

Freeze?

DR. HOENIKKER
And all the puddles in the frozen muck?

GENERAL
They'd freeze!

DR. HOENIKKER
And all the pools in the frozen muck?

MISS MARTIN
They'd freeze!

DR. HOENIKKER
And all the streams in the frozen muck?

GENERAL

[*Shouting*]

They'd freeze!

DR. HOENIKKER

   [*Shouting*]

You bet your bottom dollar they would.

STONY

   [*Dismally, under his breath*]

Hooray . . .

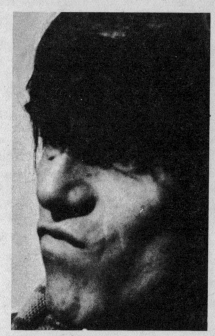

GENERAL
And the marines would rise from the swamp and march on. That's it. That's just what I need, doctor. Oh, wait'll the Pentagon hears about this. It'll be the biggest thing since air transport. . . . Merry Christmas, girls.

[*Girl pool choruses "Merry Christmas"*]

[*Girl pool exits singing "We Wish You A Merry Christmas"*]

GENERAL
I'll let you know Monday how much I can finagle for the pilot studies. You know, doctor, before we're through, I've got a feeling that you're going to turn out to be another Einstein.

[*General exits humming the "Marine Hymn"*]

[*Silence*]

STONY
There really isn't any Ice Nine, *is* there?

DR. HOENIKKER
Not yet.

STONY
I mean, if the streams were frozen in the swamp, what about the rivers the streams fed?

DR. HOENIKKER
They'd freeze, too . . . but there is no such thing.

STONY
And the oceans the frozen rivers fed?

DR. HOENIKKER

[*Beginning to get angry*]

They'd freeze . . . what are you after, young man?

STONY
And the springs feeding the frozen lakes and streams, and all the water underground feeding the springs?

DR. HOENIKKER
They'd freeze.

STONY
And the rain?

DR. HOENIKKER
When it fell, it would freeze—

STONY
—into little hard hobnails of Ice Nine . . . and that would be the end of the world . . . .

DR. HOENIKKER
Damn it all, yes.

STONY
You should have told him that.

[STONY's *face distorts into a blue mask. His face rolls over itself again and again. Cut to Mission Control and the continuing television coverage.*]

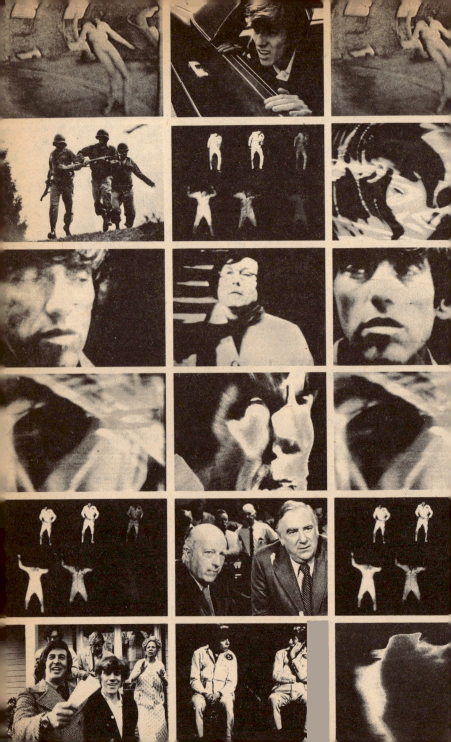

GESUNDHEIT

Due to the lull here in information from outer space, Bud, right now . . . I was thinking you, as our resident expert, could answer a few of the questions that have been sent in here to Mission Control from air viewers all over the country—

WILLIAMS
Sure thing, Walter.

GESUNDHEIT
—if we can prevail upon you for a few moments. This first one here is from little Susan, age ten, of Kenosha, Wisconsin. She says, "I love Stony. He is cute. Does he have a girl friend?"

WILLIAMS
No, I don't believe he does at the present time.

GESUNDHEIT
From San Francisco, Mr. R. L. says—asks, "When does Stony—" It appears to be incomplete.

WILLIAMS
"Shave," probably, is what he means. There is a time in the program once a day when we shave, just as there's a time to eat our meal, and so forth.

GESUNDHEIT
Well, now tell me, as long as you were out in space yourself, did you have any favorite foods?

WILLIAMS
Yes, dehydrated artichoke hearts were a favorite for me. The creamed turkey was very good, too.

GESUNDHEIT
And Tang . . .

WILLIAMS
Of course.

[*Distorted image of* STONY *appears. A gun is pointed at him.*]

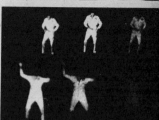

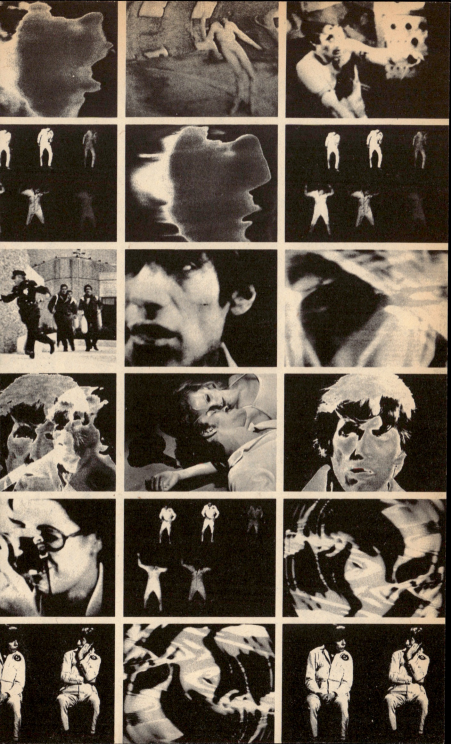

POLICEMAN

[*To* STONY]

Don't get smart, buster. I can pull a trigger as well as anybody.

[*Sound of gun. Gunshot hits fire alarm. Bells ring. Handicapped vigilantes chase* STONY.]

VOICE OF DIANA MOON GLAMPERS
Insist on your right to be equal! Under the two hundred and forty-third, and two hundred and forty-fourth, and two hundred and fifty-fifth amendments to our Constitution, it is the law of that land that nobody can be better looking than you are . . . nobody can be smarter than you are . . . nobody can run faster than you can . . .

DIANA MOON GLAMPERS

How do you do. I am Diana Moon Glampers, your handicapper general. If you know of anyone who can do something better than you can, it is your duty to report that person to my office at once. We want to handicap him fast, so he won't make you or anybody feel inferior ever again. Wherever you live, no matter what time of day or night, simply dial one-seven-seven-six. Tell the operator who it is that's making you feel like something the cat drug in. We'll cream him. We'll settle his hash.

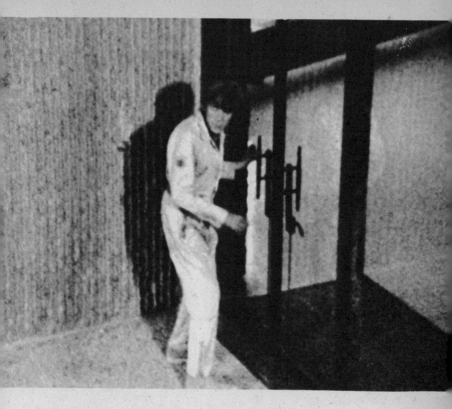

[STONY *eludes his enemies. He finds himself trapped in a television studio.*]

FIRST STAGEHAND
Wow! Wh-wh-where's your ha-ha-ha-handicaps?

STONY
What?

FIRST STAGEHAND
G-g-g-g-g-et this g-g-guy some ha-ha-ha-handicaps!
G-g-g-get this guy some handicaps!

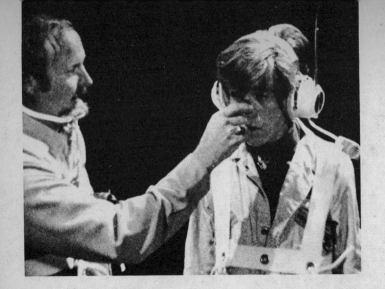

LARRY
Here you. Take this! Put it on and be quick about it!

STONY
What is this? You're making a mistake. . . .

LARRY
You're one for the books, you are. . . .

FIRST STAGEHAND
Come on wise guy . . . into your handicaps.

[*They strap sandbags on* STONY]

LARRY
I've got two twenty-five pounders on the front, Mike.

FIRST STAGEHAND
And two forty pounders on the back.

LARRY
That ought to slow you down, mac.

FIRST STAGEHAND
Hey, meathead . . . what's your IQ?

STONY
Oh, maybe a hundred and thirty-one.

LARRY
A hundred and thirty-one! Jeez, you gotta get a radio! Mike, you got a spare?

FIRST STAGEHAND
Right . . . get it right away.

STONY
Why do I need a radio?

LARRY
Well, it's only fair, ain't it? I mean, it stands to reason: you got more brains than most, so you need a radio so you don't take advantage of everybody.

[*Stagehand puts headsets on* STONY]

FIRST STAGEHAND
Here, put this on quick and you better get outta here . . . here comes the director. . . .

[LARRY *puts false nose on* STONY]

LARRY
And wear this, too.

[*Awful noise hits headsets.* STONY *staggers with the sound*]

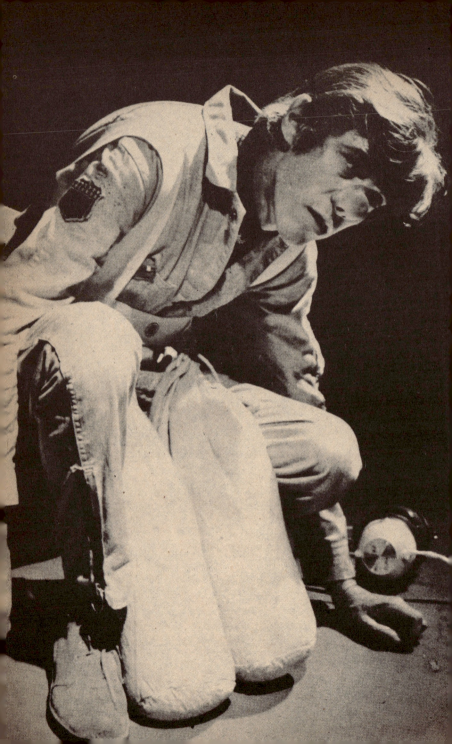

DIANA MOON GLAMPERS

Anyone tampering with government IQ handicap radio will be subject to two years in prison or a fine of ten thousand dollars in compliance with article three-three-four-J. Hate that superior intellect of yours!

   [*Noise of headsets gets louder*]

That'll settle its hash!

   [STONY *throws off headsets. He hears tapping of* DIRECTOR'S *cane*]

STAGEHANDS

   [*To* DIRECTOR]

Good day, sir. Hello, Mr. Director.

   [*We see blindfolded TV* DIRECTOR *being led by seeing-eye dog*]

[*TV music up full*]

NEWS ANNOUNCER
And now direct from Television City, the home of the big shows . . . we bring you . . .

[*Music swells*]

. . . Television City's Symphonette under the baton of Alfred Bluejean . . .

[*Music swells*]

. . . presenting Television City's own Corps de Ballet in a special performance of Musical Moments.

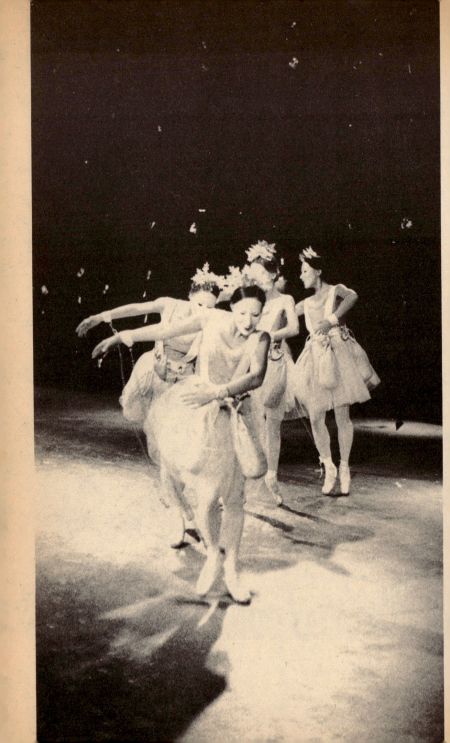

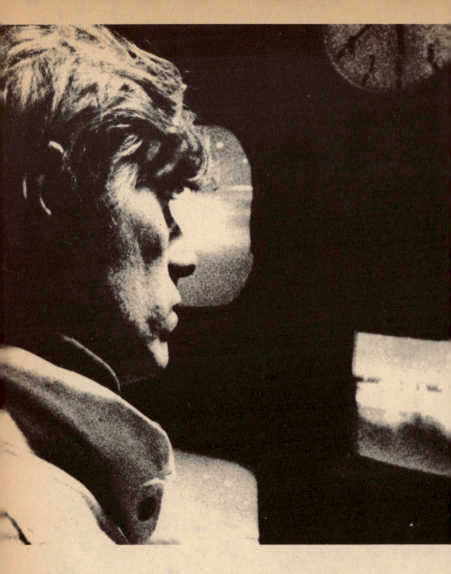

[STONY *gets rid of handicaps and hides in deserted television control room*]

[*Music is interrupted*]

NEWS ANNOUNCER
Good evening, ladies and gentlemen. This is a
. . . uh . . . We're interrupting this program
because of a . . . special news bulletin which has
just come in.

   [*He looks for the bulletin*]

Ladies and gentlemen, the police have announced
today that Harry . . . Berger?

   [*He removes thick glasses for a moment to read
   name*]

Harrison Bergeron, age twenty-three, was being
held on . . .

   [*Lifts glasses again*]

suspicion of conspiracy. Bergeron is a genius and
an athlete and is considered very dangerous.

[*Music resumes*]

NEWS ANNOUNCER
We had that story about Harrison Bergeron, and we forgot to show you his picture. Here is a picture of Harrison Bergeron, ladies and gentlemen.

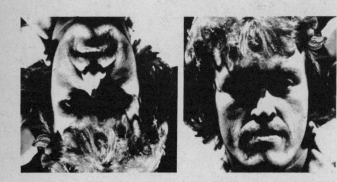

Harrison Bergeron is considered very dangerous. So shoot first. That's all from the police. Good evening.

[*Ballet resumes, but is interrupted by entrance of strange handicapped figure. It is* HARRISON BERGERON. *He breaks out of his handicaps.*]

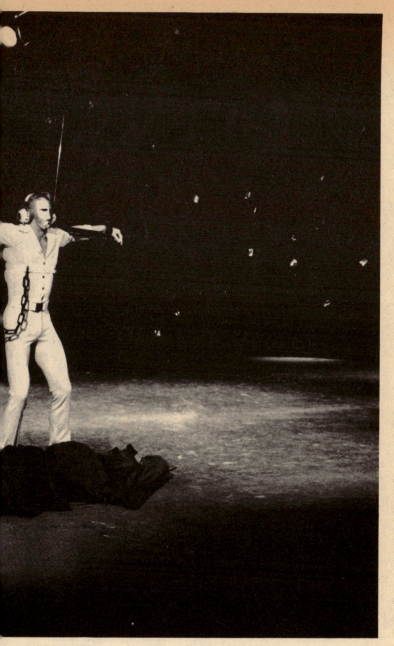

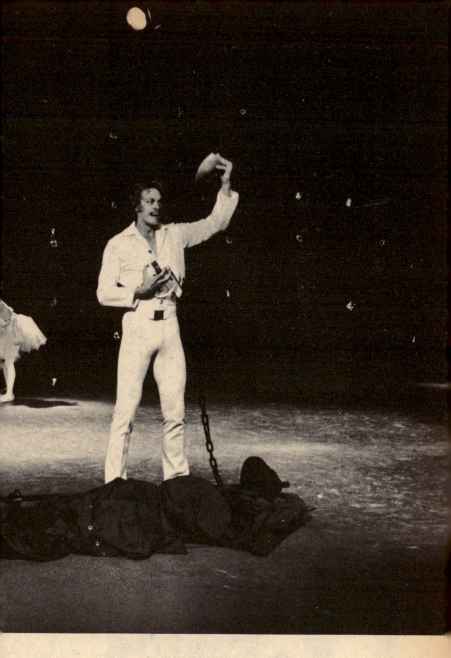

HARRISON BERGERON

[*To* BALLERINAS]

Who will dance with me?

HARRISON BERGERON
YOU!

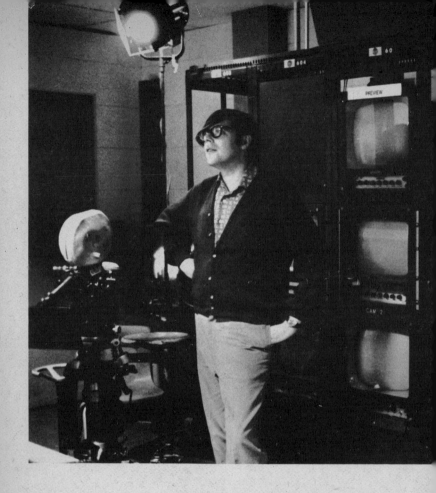

VOICE OF TV DIRECTOR

[*On P.A.*]

This is your director speaking. I must advise you
to stop what you are doing. It is totally against
the law. I cannot be responsible for what happens
to you. Really, you must stop this immediately!
Won't you stop . . .

[HARRISON BERGERON *removes ballerina's handicaps*]

HARRISON BERGERON
Music!

[*The strains of "Romeo and Juliet" fill the air. They dance.*]

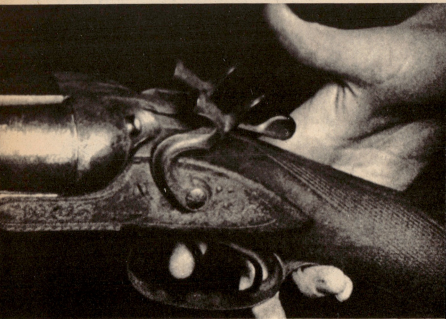

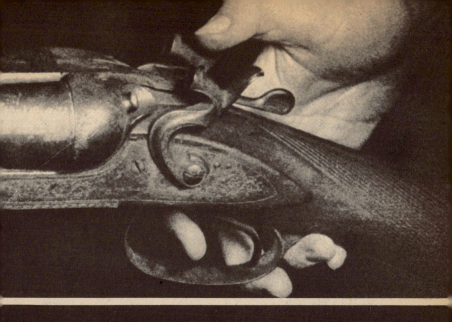

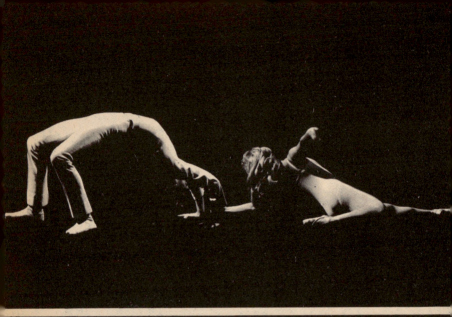
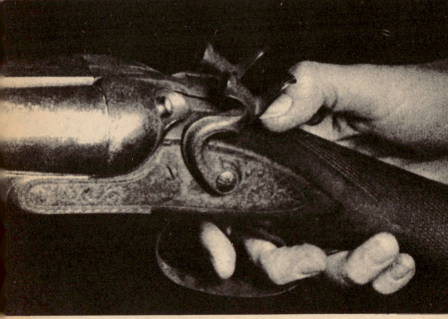

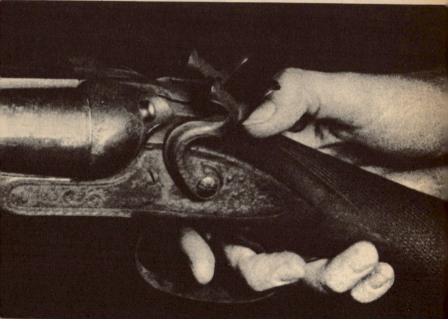

[Sound of rifle shot. The dancers fall in slow motion to the ground in a pool of blood. GLAMPERS *arrives carrying smoking double shotgun.]*

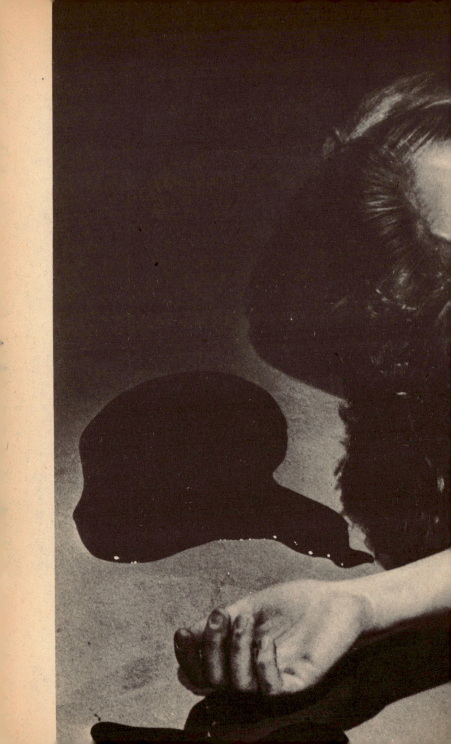

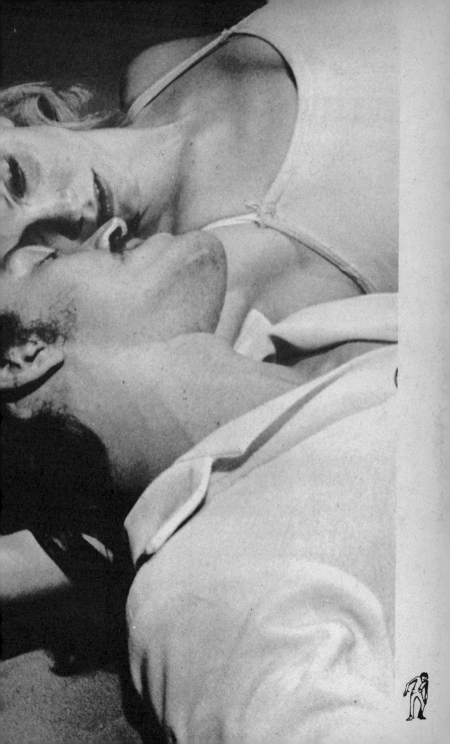

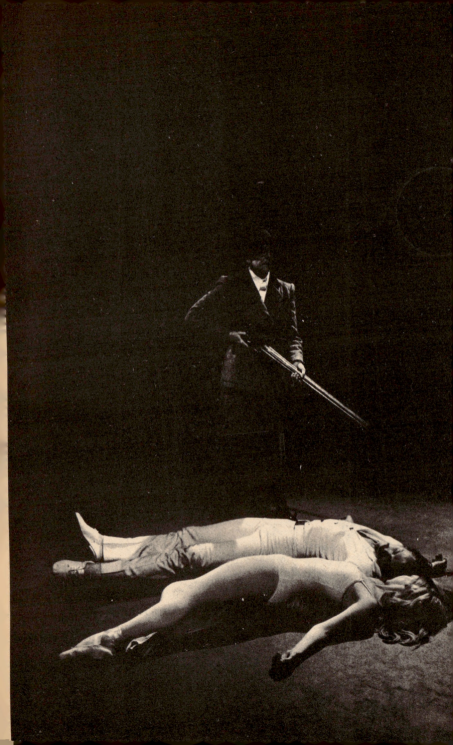

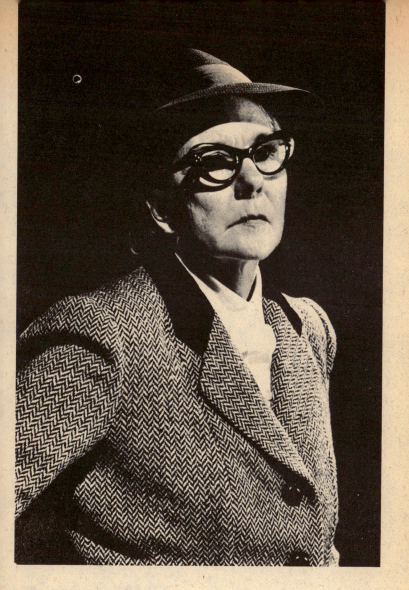

DIANA MOON GLAMPERS
Some of the TV shows they put on nowadays are downright indecent!

[STONY's *image cascades through
an eternity of distortions.
Sad music fills the air.*]

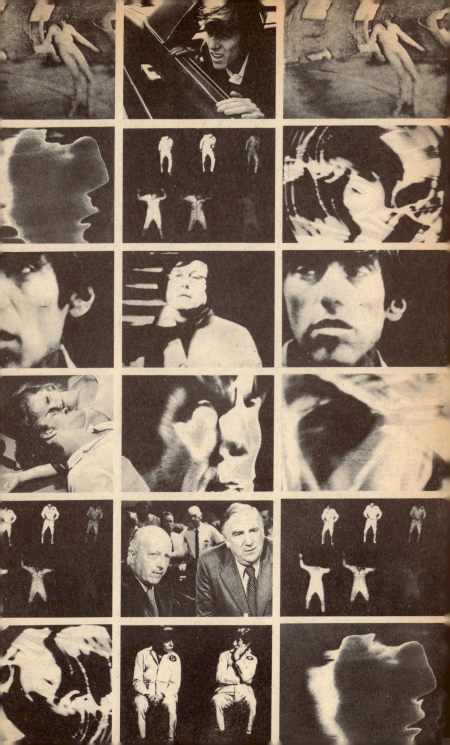

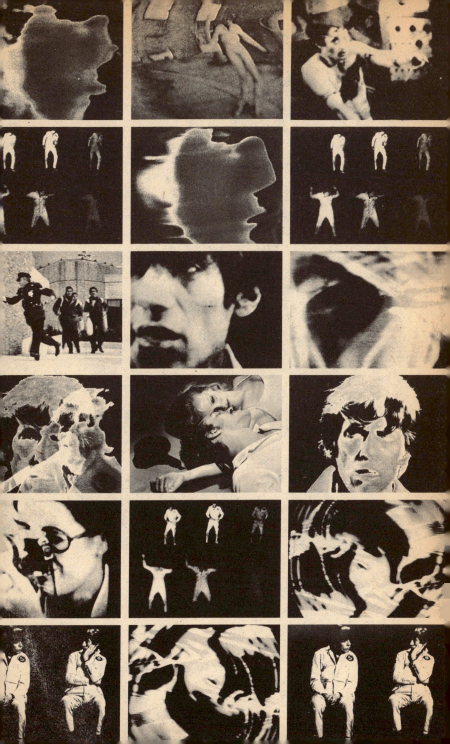

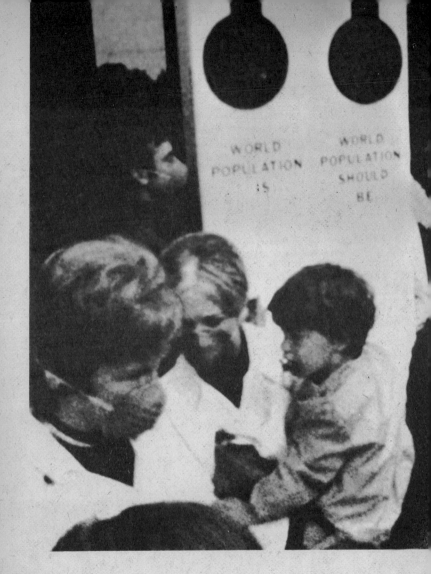

VOICE OVER

Forty-three billion babies were born last year.
The earth's population doubles every two months.
Eight million people die from suffocation every

day. If all the four-year-old children on earth
were placed end to end, they would reach the sun.
The oceans of the earth have shrunk to one-eighth
the size they were ten years ago. . . .

SHORT ORDER COOK
It's always stone cold by the time the client takes the first bite. He isn't going to eat much more than the first bite anyway. Appetite isn't a big problem over there.

[*Indicating tray, which is ready*]

All right—take this over to—uh—

[*Checking the order*]

Howard—Mr. Lionel J. Howard.

STONY
Lionel J. Howard.

SHORT ORDER COOK
Don't worry about carrying disease. You're carrying food to the Ethical Suicide Parlor. You could have bubonic plague and it wouldn't make any difference to the people over there. They'll all be dead in an hour anyway.

[STONY *fights his way through throngs of people packed together like sardines. He enters a quiet motel-like establishment. He approaches a beautiful hostess who is rushing up the stairs.*]

Drop in
and
Turn off
today

NANCY
You're late.

STONY
Sorry. I've got this—this thing about time.

NANCY
You're new.

STONY
Yes.

NANCY

You are not only late—but you are not smiling enough. One ought never let that smile fade when he is in here.

    [STONY *smiles*]

Wider!

    [STONY *smiles wider*]

Follow me.

STONY

What are all the people doing outside?

NANCY

What kind of a question is that? They're living.

STONY

Oh.

NANCY

Isn't any more crowded out there than it is anyplace else. You know anyplace that's any *less* crowded?

STONY

Nope.

NANCY

All right. Mr. Howard is right in there. You give him his meal, and you listen very politely to whatever he has to say. He's got a lot to say.

STONY

Can do.

NANCY

If he suddenly decides it's time to die, agree with him strongly—ring the bell, and keep him in a suicidal frame of mind till I get there.

STONY

Right.

NANCY

And smile . . .

[STONY *knocks on door*]

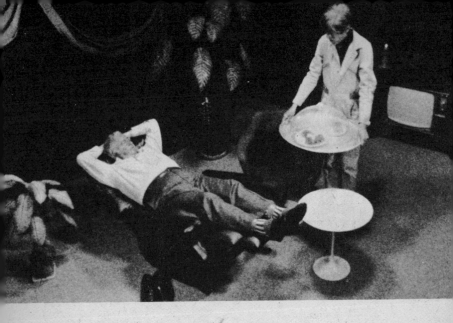

LIONEL J. HOWARD
Don't be shy. Come in! Come in! And wipe that idiotic grin off your face. That's part of your job—smile, smile, smile. You think I don't know that?

STONY
I brought your food.

LIONEL J. HOWARD
Put it on the table and sit down. Nice to get away from the crowd. Think a lot of people would like your job—the opportunity to get into a suicide parlor without dying, but getting away from the crowd.

STONY
I'm lucky, I guess.

LIONEL J. HOWARD
Human beings are like drupelets now.

STONY

Drupelets?

LIONEL J. HOWARD

The little knobs on a raspberry—those are drupelets. Now human beings are jammed together like that. What took you so long?

STONY

Just general ineptitude—some character flaws.

LIONEL J. HOWARD

Another two minutes of waiting for you, and I'd have walked out of here.

STONY

You would have decided to . . . to go on living?

LIONEL J. HOWARD

You call what they're doing out there living? I don't call that living.

STONY

There must be some other word.

LIONEL J. HOWARD

I've chosen cyanide. My wife wanted me to take the carbon monoxide, God knows why. "Maude," I said, "cyanide's more masculine." When they started the Ethical Suicide Program, I wrote the president of the United States and told him that veterans should have the option of being tied to a stake with full military honors and then shot with by a firing squad of United States Marines in dress blues. I got a form letter back. He said he'd passed on my suggestion to the VA. Wound up in some bureaucrat's wastebasket, I expect.

TV ANNOUNCER
Difficult to remember, isn't it? A day without your ethical birth control pill. A day without that wonderful numb feeling below your waist, a day without . . .

STONY
What is that?

LIONEL J. HOWARD
Oh, the hostesses keep feeding those suicide commercials in here. They're loaded with lots of reasons to get the hell off earth.

TV ANNOUNCER
The beautiful pill that almost kept our population in control. The beautiful pill that helps us through the days—until the day of complete bliss arrives—the bliss of blessed death. Just peace, and your nearest Ethical Suicide Parlor. Your favorite meal from Howard Johnson's . . . served by our charming hostesses . . . in a scrumptious suicide room, where you—and you alone—can expire. Haven't you had enough? Why don't you call your local Ethical Suicide Parlor today? It's the ethical way to go.

LIONEL J. HOWARD
Been listening to that government stuff for years.
Never had any use for it before.

NANCY
You did say cyanide, didn't you, Mr. Howard?

LIONEL J. HOWARD
I've said a lot of things in this vale of tears.
Somewhere in there I must have said—cyanide.

NANCY
It's time.

LIONEL J. HOWARD
Could I see the suicide commercials again?

NANCY
Oh, Mr. Howard, you know these all by heart.

LIONEL J. HOWARD
You know, I once saw this experiment that the government ran to test the effectiveness of the ethical birth control pill, to see if a man who took one could feel anything below the waist. They blindfolded a guy and then gave him the Gettysburg Address. Right in the middle of the recitation they kicked him real hard, right where it hurts—and he never missed a syllable. I get to ask one last question.

NANCY
You what?

LIONEL J. HOWARD
I get to ask one last question, and you have to give me a truthful answer to it. That's the law.

NANCY
I never heard of that law. Oh, Mr. Howard, you're making that up.

LIONEL J. HOWARD
I swear it's the law.

NANCY

   [*To* STONY]

A lot of 'em start making up new laws when it gets to be near the end.

LIONEL J. HOWARD
Why not?

NANCY
Mr. Howard, shall we ask for the needle now?

LIONEL J. HOWARD
If you'll answer my question.

NANCY
I'll make a bargain with you. You ask for the needle. I'll give you the needle. Then you ask the question, and I'll answer as best I can.

LIONEL J. HOWARD
All right. The needle, please.

NANCY

   [*Withdrawing needle deftly*]

There you are.

LIONEL J. HOWARD
Yes sir . . . while he was reciting the Gettysburg Address, they kicked him right in the ba . . .

   [LIONEL J. HOWARD *groans softly, loses consciousness*]

STONY
He—he never got to ask his question.

NANCY
Oh, that's all right. He'll wake up in about ten seconds. He can ask it then.

[LIONEL J. HOWARD *stirs and looks toward* STONY]

NANCY
I believe he wants to put the question to you. You won't have time to answer.

[STONY *leans close.* LIONEL J. HOWARD *tries again and again to phrase his question, finally gets it out*]

LIONEL J. HOWARD
What . . . what are people—for?

[LIONEL J. HOWARD *dies*]

[*Dissolve to long line of candles quietly flickering. The music is sad and slow.*]

[*Scene changes to* STONY *with kitten on flat dry ground in wide empty arena at night*]

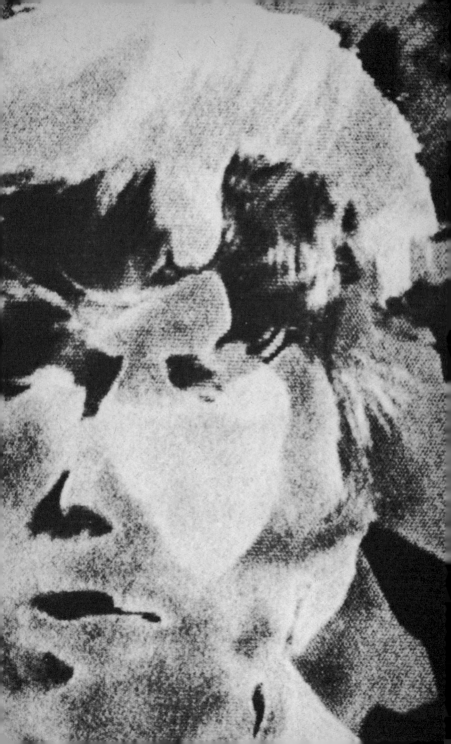

GIRL'S VOICE

In the beginning, God created the Earth, and he said, "Let there be mud." And there was mud. And God said, "Let Us make living creatures out of mud, so the mud can see what We have done." And God created every living creature that now moveth, and one was man. Mud-as-man alone could speak.

   [STONY *bends over to pet cat*]

    What is the purpose of all this?" man asked politely.
   "Everything must have a purpose?" asked God.
   "Certainly," said man.

   [*Cat walks away*]

   "Then I leave it to you to think of one for all of this," said God. And He went away.

[*Scene changes to* STONY *hitchhiking*]

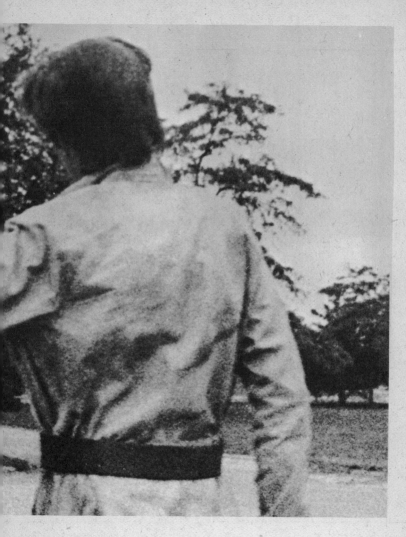

[*Noise of vehicle approaching.* WANDA JUNE *appears on firetruck*]

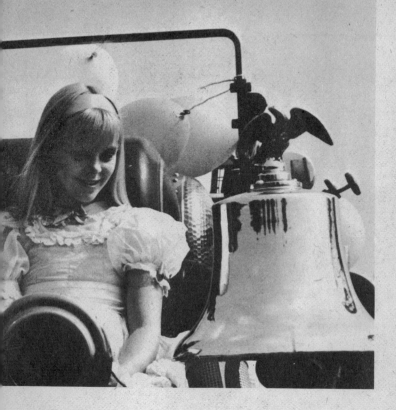

WANDA JUNE
Hi. Room for one more.

STONY
Am I dead?

WANDA JUNE
Nothing to be ashamed about. Hold on! Here we go . . . !

WANDA JUNE

I am Wanda June. Today was going to be my birthday, but I was hit by an ice-cream truck before I could have my party. I am dead now. I am in Heaven. I am not mad at the ice-cream truck driver, even though he was drunk when he hit me. It didn't hurt much. It wasn't even as bad as the sting of a bumblebee. I am really happy here! It's so much fun. I am glad the driver was drunk. If he hadn't been, I might not have got to Heaven for years and years and years. I would have had to go to high school first, and then beauty college. I would have had to get married and have babies and everything. Everybody up here is happy—the animals and the dead soldiers and people who went to the electric chair and everything. They're all glad for whatever sent them here. Nobody is mad. We're all too busy playing shuffleboard. So if you think of killing somebody, don't worry about it. Just go ahead and do it. Whoever you do it to should kiss you for doing it. The soldiers up here just love the shrapnel and the tanks and the bayonets and the dumdums that let them play shuffleboard all the time—and drink beer.

[*Carnival music. Noises of happy crowd. The crowd moves into a large arena celebrating the arrival of* STONY.]

[*The music comes to a discordant end as Hitler appears, goosestepping and snarling from the balcony.*]

HITLER
What a poor specimen of a man you are.

STONY
That's been said before.

HITLER
Do you know who I am?

STONY
Yes. And you scare the hell out of me. I think you scare me more than anything I've ever seen in my life.

HITLER
I am death, and I am here to tell you all there is to know about me.

STONY

   [*Shaking his head uncertainly*]

I don't think so.

HITLER

   [*Drawing himself up*]

You deny I am death?

STONY
I think you're my childhood dream of the most terrible creature that could ever be.

   [*Looking around*]

And I think that this is my childhood dream of how God might try to make everybody happy when they were dead.

HITLER
I am death, and I am final.

  [*Aside, awed by himself*]

God, am I ever final.

  [*To* STONY]

When I say the magic word to all these people,
they will vanish forever. I will then say the
magic words to you, and you, too, will vanish—
never to be seen again.

  [*To the crowd, horrifyingly*]

There is no Heaven!
When you are dead, you are dead. That's all
there is to it.
There is no afterlife in any way . . .

  [*One-third of the crowd vanishes*]

Shape!

[*Another one-third of the crowd vanishes*]

Or form!

[*Only* STONY *and* WANDA JUNE *are left*]

Go to the worms, you fool!

WANDA JUNE

[*Pitifully*]

The worms?

HITLER
To the worms, my blond, Teutonic child.

WANDA JUNE

[*Bleakly*]

Good-bye.

HITLER
Good-bye!
And then there was one.

STONY

[*Half to himself, a growing insight*]

Death in inner space.

HITLER

[*Sniffing insubordination*]

What's this?

[STONY *touches his head*]

STONY

It's all up here . . . you . . . them . . . this . . . Mission Control . . . the moon, the sun, the stars.

[*Growing stronger, a good man forced unwillingly into a test of strength, supposing, after all, that he might just win*]

I am going to make *you* disappear.

HITLER

> [*Bluffing, hoping he isn't bluffing*]

How?

STONY

> [*Bowing his head, patting it all over, familiarizing himself with a powerful weapon he has only now recognized as a weapon*]

Up there! I'll use this up here!

> [*Raising his head, nearly ready for a test*]

There *is* an afterlife, if I create one up here. I can create anything up here . . .

> [*Meaning death,* HITLER]

or destroy it.

> [STONY *and* HITLER *square off like wrestlers*]

HITLER

> [*With mock lightness*]

Life against death?

STONY
Death against . . . imagination.

HITLER

[*Suddenly striking the first magical blow, not touching* STONY, *but closing his eyes and writhing with incredible body English, wishing him out of existence with all of his might.*]

Disappear! Disappear! Disappear!

[STONY *writhes, sinks to his knees, rises again, refuses at great cost to disappear.* HITLER *opens his eyes, sees that* STONY *has survived, becomes an old man of putty, such as* HITLER *became at the end of World War II.*]

So.

STONY

[*With a gentle, sure gesture, quietly*]

Disappear.

[HITLER *disappears*]

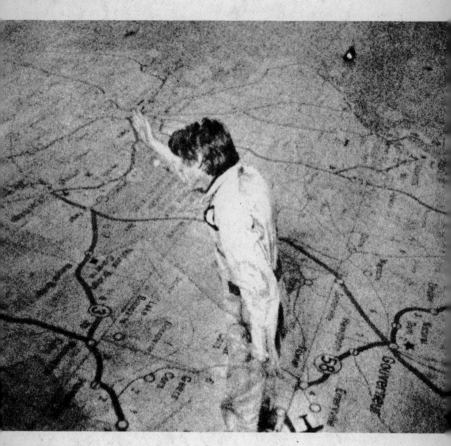

[STONY *alone, gestures*]

Appear!

   [*Crowd appears in front of* STONY]

Disappear!

   [STONY *alone*]

Appear!

[*Crowd appears*]

Disappear!

[STONY *alone*]

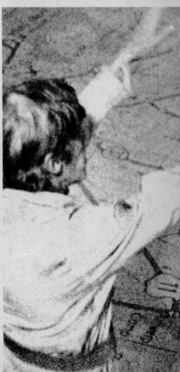

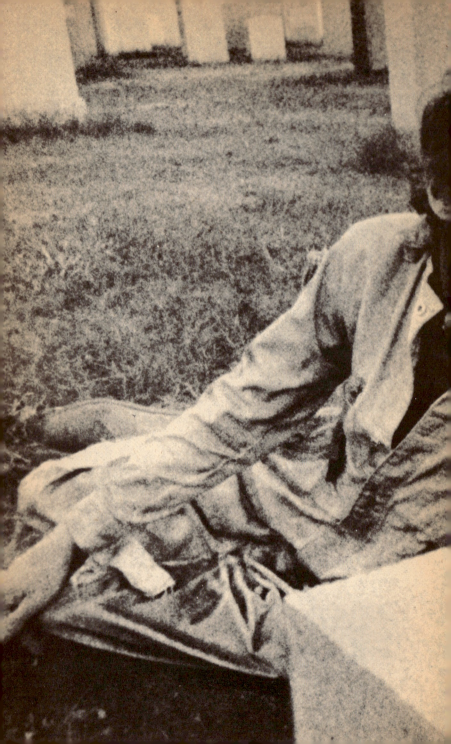

[STONY *working his way out of grave in Brooklyn cemetery*]

STONY

[*Reading epitaph on tombstone*]

"Stony Stevenson, Astronaut. Everything was beautiful and nothing hurt." Oh, lucky me. Lucky mud.

VOICE OF BOKONON
See what a nice job God has done.

STONY

[*Hearing* BOKONON'S *voice inwardly*]

Nice going, God. I certainly couldn't have done it. I feel very unimportant compared to you.

VOICE OF BOKONON
The only way you can feel the least bit important is to think of all the mud that didn't even get to sit up and look around.

STONY

> [*Standing up, wiping some of the earth from his space suit*]

I got so much, and most mud got so little.
"What's the use of worrying . . . it never was
  worthwhile   . .
So pack up your troubles in an old kit bag and
  smile, smile, smile"

[STONY *walks away from grave and approaches a man with a lawn mower. Noise of lawn mower. Noise stops*]

STONY

[*Pointing back at his own tomb*]

There's a tombstone back there . . .

CEMETERY GARDENER

A tombstone! An understatement is what that is.

STONY

It says, "Stony Stevenson, Astronaut."

CEMETERY GARDENER

He's not actually buried there, of course. That's just a memorial his mother put up. He's out in space or he's out in time. Who knows where he is?

STONY

Right. You know, it says on the stone . . .

CEMETERY GARDENER

"Everything was beautiful and nothing hurt?"

   [STONY *nods*]

I thought everybody knew that.

STONY

I've been away.

CEMETERY GARDENER

His space capsule splashed down in the Pacific, right on target. But when they opened it up, it was empty. There was just a note in there, and a half-finished bottle of Tang. And the note said what's on the tombstone.

STONY

Thank you.

CEMETERY GARDENER

Any time.

[*He restarts his lawn mower.* STONY *walks through the cemetery*]

"What the use of worrying? It never was
  worthwhile . . .
So pack up your troubles in an old kit bag,
And smile . . . smile . . . smile . . ."

Between TIME and TIMBUKTU

AN NET PLAYHOUSE SPECIAL

Produced by
DAVID LOXTON

Directed by
FRED BARZYK

Adapted for television by
FRED BARZYK
DAVID LOXTON
DAVID ODELL

Associate Producers
MATTHEW N. HERMAN
OLIVIA TAPPAN

Director of Photography
BOYD ESTUS

Sound
WIL MORTON

Editor
DICK BARTLETT

Casting
ARNOLD HOSKWITH

Costume Designer
PATTON CAMPBELL

Sets
FRANCIS MAHARD
CLINT HEITMAN

Assistant Costume Designer
PENELOPE BELKNAP

Choreography
WILMA CURLEY

Special Video Effects
DAVID ATWOOD

Gaffer
JOHN MACKNIGHT

Assistant Cameraman and Grip
ROGER HAYDOCK

Assistant Editor
STEVE SHANE

Stock Footage
DELL BYRNE

Graphics
EUGENE MACKELS

Additional Sound
DAVE LOERZEL

Music Consultant
JOHN Q. ADAMS

Production Manager
ELIZABETH O. DAVIS

Animated film designed by
RON FINDLAY
GAIL GUTRADT

Animated film produced by
Folio One Productions Ltd.

Supervision
AL BRODAX

Animator
MARTON OMMUNDSEN

Production Assistants
JANET OLIVER
TOM QUINN
PETE SCOON

Our thanks to Elkins Productions
International Corporation for
permission to include excerpts
from the novel *Cat's Cradle*

Our thanks to
Air & Space Gyro Services
Eastern Benson Gyro
The Holy Child Marching One Hundred
Massachusetts General Hospital
Massachusetts Metropolitan District Commission
Museum of Science, Boston
New York City Parks and Recreation Department
Paik-Abe Synthesiser
Queens Day Preparatory School
Quincy Market Cold Storage
Utility Supply Company
And lots of friends

Executive Producer
JAC VENZA

A Production of
NET
in collaboration with
WGBH Boston

WGBH's participation was made possible by grants from the **Ford Foundation** and the **Rockefeller Foundation**

PHOTO CREDITS

JILL KREMENTZ: 1; 2; 3; 5; 6; 7; 8–9; 10 (*all*); 11; 13; 16 (*all*); 17; 22; 26; 27; 28 (*both lower R*); 30 (*Top, 3rd from top*); 31 (*2nd and 3rd from top*); 32 (*Top, 3rd from top*); 33 (*Top*); 36; 37 (*all*); 38 (*all*); 39 (*all*); 42–3; 46; 48; 49; 50–1; 52; 54; 55; 56–7; 58; 60 (*Top, 2nd from bottom*); 61 (*4th row R*); 62 (*Bottom C*); 63 (*Bottom R, top C*); 64 (*Top L and R, 2nd row C, 3rd row L, bottom C*); 65 (*2nd row L, 3rd row C, bottom L*); 68; 70–1; 72; 74–5; 76–7; 78; 79 (*Bottom*); 82; 83 (*all*); 84 85; 88; 92 (*Top*); 93 (*2nd from top, 4th from top*); 96 (*Top C, 2nd row L, 4th row C, bottom L*); 97 (*4th row C*); 132–3 (*same as pages 96–7*); 138; 150 (*Bottom*); 151; 152 (*2nd from top*); 153 (*Bottom*); 156–7 (*same as pages 96–7*); 158; 160–1 (*same as pages 96–7*); 166; 168; 170; 171; 172–3; 174–5; 176; 177; 178; 180; 181; 182; 183; 184–5; 186 (*Bottom L and R*); 187; 188; 189; 190–1; 192–3; 194–5; 196–7; 198; 199; 200–1; 202–3; 204–5; 206; 207; 208 (*Top*); 209 (*all*); 210; 211 (*Bottom*); 212 (*Top*); 213; 214; 215 (*Top*); 216–7; 218–9; 220; 221; 223 (*Top C, 4th row L, 5th row C*); 224–5 (*same as pages 96–7*); 250–1; 252.

NASA: 18 (*all*); 19 (*all*); 20; 21; 35; 40–1; 44–5; 278; 282; 284.

All other photos are from the NET Playhouse production.